tHe souL ListeneR

the
SOUL
Listener

m'basen wazir

EsArpi

2007

EsArpi

EsArpi Publishing
P.O. Box 51, Gananoque, Ontario CANADA K7G 1G5
www.esarpi.com

National Library of Canada Cataloguing in Publication Data

Wazir, M'basen,
    The soul listener / M'basen Wazir.

ISBN-13 978-0-9781957-2-4

    1. Guardian angels—Fiction. I. Title.

PS8645.A95S63 2007   C813'.6   C2007-905182-0

For everyone

INtRODUCtION

I hesitated to write this little blurb that would serve as the introduction to *The Soul Listener* for various reasons.

First, I'm not convinced that author introductions are actually read or particularly interesting. Sometimes, it's just the author listing everybody he or she needs to thank and so on and so on. Next, it's supposed to be the place where the author gives the reader a glimpse into the incredible creative journey undertaken which ultimately culminated in the published work.

I'm not sure what would be accomplished if I carried on about either.

I'd rather not list individuals who helped in bringing this work to completion. They are many. Instead, thanks to all. Thanks to those who had a positive influence on me in one way or another at various times in my life. Also, thanks to those who have had a negative impact on me in one way or another; you have helped me more than you know.

However, notwithstanding I have nothing of relative importance to say here, I did decide to write an introduction, the majority of which you have just read. But now, when it comes right down to it—to what one should say in an introduction—I have no idea what to say. I've said what I had to say in the novel. If at some point something else comes to mind that I need to get off my chest, then I suppose I could write another little book with which to say it. That, however, will have to wait for another day.

If I may, I'd like to backtrack slightly on one of my earlier stances. I would like to thank Janice Van Eck. Without her involvement in this project, this story now called *The Soul Listener* would never have become a book. Rather, it would have remained just a story; just a bunch of words posing as my first manuscript that I had banished to the bottom of a milk crate in the trunk of my car. So, to her, thank you.

In conclusion, I will offer this.

Listen. Listen to your soul, your hunches, your head, your heart, people around you, opportunities, successes and failures. Then, after listening, make your own decisions. Don't let the noise of the planet influence you for no good reason. You see, life sometimes prevents goals and dreams; but blindly followed goals and dreams sometimes prevent destinies. And that—a destiny—is what is inside every human, trying to get out. No, *screaming* to get out. Listen for it. It's there.

M'basen Wazir

I

DOC

Doc smiled.

He had just passed his Senior Theory exams and, he was remembering, rather fondly, how his faith, belief in himself, belief in his silent partner and hard work had also worked out for him Below. But he was Above now.

It was a clear, bright day in Heaven—really, how would there be anything but? It's said that clear days are all there are Above, save for two short periods some time ago. One, on part of the First Day before God created Light. And two, some years later, from the time of the Death on the Friday until the Resurrection Sunday.

So, the day when Doc, a young Guardian Angel, met—well, wandered upon—St. Michael, the Archangel, the greatest of all

Angels, was just another typical day in Heaven. Clear, with a comforting breeze just slight enough to calmly brush a smiling cheek and warm enough to gently content the heart.

Doc, a new—so to speak—young—relatively—eager Guardian Angel had just found out he passed his Senior Theory exams. And with that discovery also came news of his impending promotion from Junior to the rank of Senior Guardian Angel. However, he would still have to pass his Senior Observational Interviews before he would get his new assignment Below and be classified as a full-fledged Senior Guardian Angel. For the time being he would be an official Senior Candidate.

I'm ready for my next challenge, he thought, as he walked along a smaller path he turned onto that forked off The Main Path some distance from the Academy grounds where he had just been granted his new rank.

This is great, thought Doc. Similar to being watered and fed, I guess…but not completely the same. Similar in the sense of accomplishment and fulfillment. But I think the similarity ends there.

He entered the Academy that day a Junior and now later, he was walking out the Academy's front doors a Senior Candidate. Doc was beaming like a schoolboy—which, technically, he was—as he walked home. He still didn't know who his next assignment would be Below nor did he know who would be his examiner—the Angel who would oversee his Observational Interviews. No, all Doc knew was that he was embarking on a new challenge.

As Doc walked home he thought that the sun was particularly bright and the birds more cheerful. They seem happy too. Maybe they're happy for me.

"I'm a Senior Candidate you know," Doc said in his quiet unassuming voice to a chickadee that was perched right at eye level on a young oak tree a few feet off the path.

Doc kept walking and hummed one of his favourite songs "Given to Fly" as he turned on to yet another smaller path that brought him closer to home. Without a soul in sight and no one to tell his good news Doc kept striding towards home on the network of little paths that branched off The Main Path. As he glanced down at the little chickweed sprouting up between the cobblestones of the path, it reminded him of the odd weed he had to relocate out of his garden. I think it might be a good day to do some gardening, Doc thought, as he pulled the weed from the cobblestone path and placed it on the two-wheeled cart parked just off to the side of the path at the next fork.

The cart would then be taken to a designated area and the weeds off-loaded. Everything Above, had its spot.

2

tHe aRCHaNgeL

"Hello, Doc," St. Michael started cheerfully.

Michael—the Archangel, the greatest of all Angels, the victor foretold of in the Apocalypse, he who is like God—was sitting on a bench just off to the side where Doc was walking. Holding a chipmunk, Michael was conversing with it—as he and his many chipmunk friends did from time to time—about the nutritious virtues of black sunflower seeds as compared to striped sunflower seeds. This was serious stuff to Edmund, Michael's little furry friend. After all, what better way to know what seeds to pack away in one's hole for the winter than to seek the advice of the Archangel?

"Yo, Doc," Michael said again while never averting his eyes from nor breaking conversation with Edmund.

Doc, as he walked by the Archangel, looked like he was aware of who was sitting just off the path—if one were watching—but he didn't. He was walking one way but his mind was wandering elsewhere.

I'm a Senior, Doc thought, and in record time too. I don't know if I'm ready for this. There's so much to learn. I hope I do well in the Observational Interviews. He almost walked right past the Archangel, God's Counsel. He missed the "Hello Doc" part, but he caught someone sitting on the bench saying the "Yo" bit the second time.

Finally, Doc turned to his right and in disbelief saw Michael sitting there talking to him. Doc looked over both shoulders to see if in fact it was he who the Archangel was addressing. Yup. Michael was talking to him alright.

Just as Doc turned back again and faced the Archangel he noticed that Michael was gently lowering a chipmunk to the ground and was wishing it goodbye as it hurried on its way. "Now, Edmund," Michael laughed, "easy on the striped sunflower seeds or you'll put on some extra ounces this winter and you won't be able to squeeze out of your hole come springtime." Michael roared with laughter. Edmund turned around, smiled, and scurried off.

"Amazing creatures, chipmunks," Michael said to Doc nonchalantly as if Doc had been there all along and finally looking up at him. "Some of my best friends are chipmunks, you know. Always hurrying about, but never, never, too busy to say hello to an old friend. Ones Below could do more of that. Yes, ah, well…for the third time, hello there."

Doc was speechless. Michael, the Archangel, he who is like God, was sitting on a bench talking to him. To him! After all, it's not often Michael will be sitting just so calling your name. Doc had seen the Archangel before, but only from a distance at official Guardian Angel gatherings and certainly he had never spoken to him. Other than seeing him at the odd gathering, Doc only knew Michael from his portrait and statue in The Corridor of Saints—a hallway in the Academy.

By far, Michael was—maybe save for God—the busiest person in Heaven; of course it went without saying that he was for sure the busiest Angel. As Archangel, God's Counsel and Presiding Member of the Inner Circle, Michael had not the time usually to chat idly with young Guardian Angels—recognized as being the best of their time or not. But for some reason, there he was, chatting idly with Edmund when Doc just happened along.

Odd, thought Doc, for such a busy person to be whiling away his time just so. "Hello, Sir," Doc managed after a second or two.

"Oh please, 'Michael' will do just fine," the Archangel said kindly. "Call me Michael. Surely you can muster up the confidence to call me Michael can't you? Just don't call me Shirley."

"Sorry Shirl...I mean Sir...ah, sorry, I mean Michael," Doc stammered. "I guess it's just a throwback from my time Below when my parents instilled in me the importance of treating your elders with respect."

"Elders?" grunted Michael. "Hmmph...dude, how old do you think I am?"

"Uh...um...I don't know," Doc said with touch of embarrassment. Wanting to change the subject he quickly asked, "How are you?"

"Oh, I'm fine, couldn't be better," Michael said. "Couldn't be better and thank you for asking. Although, I did pitch a no-hitter in the Hall of Fame baseball game this morning so my shoulder is a bit tender. Get this...I struck out the side in the third: the Babe, Ty Cobb, and Hank."

"Hank?" asked Doc bewildered, because Hank Aaron, the great home run slugger, wasn't up Here yet.

"Yeah," laughed Michael. "Mantle was injured so they, uh, called, Hank up—so to speak—if you get my meaning."

"Uh...suure," Doc replied hesitantly while managing to break a grin for the first time.

"Yes, so my shoulder is a touch off, but besides that I'm fine. I should be ready for the football game tomorrow. I hear," Michael motioned Doc closer as if to whisper something of great importance as he looked both ways to see if anyone was watching, "I hear the other side is calling up Warren Moon. Think I can beat 'im?"

"I'm sure you can," Doc said with a touch of authority even though he knew nothing of Michael's football playing skills and was still unsure of the whole conversation to begin with.

"I'll leave you tickets if you want," Michael offered. "They say it's a sell-out. Haven't a clue who 'they' are though. Dear me, that's another one of life's puzzling mysteries...they. Who are 'they'?? 'They' say this and 'they' say that. Aaanyway, they're calling for fifty million in attendance. That's not counting standing room. And then they figure on another two million hovering. Wait till He puts up the Dome. He's just waiting for Michelangelo to put the finishing touches on the blueprints. Ha! Then the hoverers will have to buy tickets. It'll increase our revenue needed to refurbish the Pearlies. Not been given a real good goin' over in some time you know."

"Why doesn't God just build the Dome Himself?" Doc asked. "He can do anything, right?"

"Yes, He can," answered Michael. "However, He is eager to see if the skills He provided Michelangelo with Below are as sharp up Here. God is always willing to let people—of all various states of existence—prove their worth, Below and up Here. He will always give you ample opportunity. It's up to you to seize it—wherever you are. You just have to believe in Him and believe in yourself."

"Same for up Here as Below?" asked Doc.

"Exactly the same," replied Michael matter of factly.

"Anyway, back to more pressing matters," Michael said as he eased back on the bench. "Leaving the Interviews aside, congratulations, young man, on being named Senior Candidate. You can justifiably be proud of your accomplishment. I'm told you did it in record time. 'Cept for me of course. But I don't think they count me for the purposes of the record. Something about being around from the Beginning when it was so-called *easier* to perform. Hogwash. Aaaaaanyway, congrats on *your* record time."

"Oh, thanks," Doc said proudly, but shyly. He did catch the

Archangel's drift though.

"So, the real question is…is…how are *you*?" Michael asked.

"Me?"

"Yeah, you," Michael replied. "It's not every day we have a Senior with under thirty years of guardianship you know. Are you ready?"

"Yes. I think so," Doc said, still a little unconvinced himself of his own answer. "I hope so. I don't know. Yes, I am."

"Which is it—yes or no? C'mon my boy, as a Senior you will need more decisiveness than that. This isn't the same boy who passed the century mark for traffic diversions is it? A number that heretofore had yet to be attained. Not even Gabriel broke ninety-five, you know. 'Course, it's true that when he was a Basic and Junior he was dealing with chariots and donkeys. Kind of hard to be traffic diversion king when most of the people Below ran faster than the carts—not to take anything away from your great accomplishment, if you get my meaning. So, are you ready or are you not?"

"Yes…I'm ready," Doc replied with a touch more confidence. "But deep down I still feel like I have so much to learn. The more I learn, the more I feel I know less. Because I realize that there's so much out there that I don't know. The more I learn, it's like there is even more to know than when I first started. Which really makes me feel like I actually know less now then when I started as a Basic. Or when I was Below and really started learning—I remember feeling the same way. But I know that's not true. I know I know more now, but I feel like I don't. Michael, there's always so much to learn isn't there? When you're Below and up Here, right?"

Michael looked at Doc. He said nothing. For a moment, he was expressionless. Not even Michael's rugged good looks and his longish, wild, curly, unruly hair could cover up his dumbfounded expression. He just sat there and stared right through Doc. Not even Doc's handsome, boyish features could deflect Michael's empty stare.

Doc looked at Michael. "Does that make any sense? Should it be that the more I know I should feel like I know less? Is that a normal feeling?"

Michael moved his head in a circle as if to follow the 'less I knows' and the 'more to knows.' He furrowed his brow, opened his eyes wide, contorted his face, shook his curly mane and rubbed his temples trying his best to follow where Doc was going.

Where is this boy's head? We've given the village idiot the rank of Senior, Michael thought. Good Lord! Oh, sorry Sir, I didn't mean to think that. Hell will pay for this little meddling. Satan, always trying to screw things up for us up Here. Lucifer be damned! He's penetrated our sanctuary. Alert the forces. Everyone ahoy! Ye must gird yourselves immediately. Sound the trumpets. Doc must be stripped of his rank forthwith. Yes, that's the answer. Convene the Inner Circle. What will God say? Oh no, what will God say.

The Archangel's brain kept screaming uncontrollably. "Michael," God would start out in that booming voice—oh, that booming voice! "Michael,"—He'll probably say my name twice for effect— "what happened here? Please......please......," He always starts off with the please...pause...please routine before He unleashes a good dose of quality control. His disappointment would be unknowable.

Michael's mind was hurting as he continued thinking how God would call him to account as Presiding Member of the Inner Circle and *de facto* absentee Headmaster of the Academy "......please, tell me, how is it that Doc, you know, the one sitting in the corner with his hat on backwards, yes that one, tell me, how is it that......hmmm, you say he's now a Senior, how so?" He always finishes His questions with the utmost calm before the fury. I can't take it. Something must be done.

Michael was sweating, almost becoming delirious. His brain was yelling silently as loud as it could.

Oh no, I could lose the title of Archangel! How did this happen!? How is it possible that this Senior could possibly think the more he knows the less he learns? Or was it the more he learns the more he knows? Yes, those were his words. Nope. Nope. That wasn't it at all. This will never do. Was it......ohhhh, it doesn't matter. This will cause a constitutional crisis on the Inner Circle...and it might cost me my job! Aaaaaahhhhhhhh!!! What the heck is this guy thinking, the little devil?

Michael turned slightly towards Doc and squinted his eyes as he gave him the once over—just to be sure he wasn't.

Michael returned to his ill-looking slumping. Edmund, having returned from his hole, was frantic.

"Michael, are you ok?" asked Doc.

"I'm fine," whimpered Michael even though his eyes had rolled back in his head and his face was of the brightest crimson. Michael's head was hanging over the back of the bench. His arms hanging at his sides, limp.

Whether Michael sounded like a bleating goat or a whimpering puppy, Doc could not tell. He continued with his dilemma after hearing Michael say he was alright. Michael continued with his silent Armageddon.

"It's kind of like a never-ending process, this guardian and learning business. Kind of like life-long learning. Just like it was Below. You never stop learning if you don't choose to, I think. Reach one level......keep going," Doc said sheepishly, with his eyes cast downward, away from Michael, not entirely sure if he was right. Doc had missed Michael's silent fall off the other side of the bench moments earlier.

The bleating goat wasn't sweating anymore. His face started to look like a face again. He was starting to regain his senses.

The Rapture can now be averted. I'll be spared the booming voice.

When Michael—mid-fall—heard Doc sum up his experiences up Here as being akin to 'life-long learning' and similar to how he learned Below he snapped out of his trance. God need not be bothered. The first constitutional crisis in generations had been side-stepped. Thank goodness! Our new Senior is no village idiot.

The nonsense about learning more and knowing less threw him. Michael—even with his all-knowing powers—would never admit to it but sometimes he could be thrown by the simplest of things.

However, he understood exactly what Doc meant when he said 'life-long learning.'

"Gee Michael, are you ok?" Doc asked again as he was peering into the pupils of Michael's eyes who now lay motionless, flat out on his back on the ground beside the bench. The crimson tide was slowly waning from the Archangel's face.

"Me? Why sure. Why do you ask?" Michael asked rather huffily as he brushed off the grass, gave his head a little flick to get the hair out of his eyes and got up as if nothing happened.

"Oh, no reason," Doc said quietly and unassumingly, as he wanted to get back to their discussion. Doc really wasn't up to the task of needling the Archangel about his momentary lapse of reason.

When grace-under-pressure-Michael finally returned to his senses he knew that this boy was good. Good enough to be an...... uh......Senior, he thought. "So," Michael started, "what was it again that you are a believer in?" not making any mention of his slide off the bench nor his obvious silly meltdown. Michael just picked up exactly where he left off just before he left the bench.

Being polite, Doc picked up at the same spot also, "...being a life-long learner," said Doc, "up Here and Below."

"Ha! Perfect!" Michael exclaimed. "See, that's one of the reasons why you're a Senior in under thirty years, because you have come to understand that learning doesn't stop just because a goal is reached or because an area of study is completed or a certain level is attained. For those who want to, learning exists not only throughout their time Below but it continues on in perpetuity up Here. Has your promotion set in yet?"

As Doc listened to Michael congratulate him on being an exceptional student and Guardian Angel, he recalled that many other instructors had been impressed with his guarding abilities as well.

But Doc didn't see it. He just stayed under the radar and worked hard. Embraced learning and listened to his soul. Below and Above. Doc didn't see himself as special. He just listened and learned what his soul taught him.

Maybe, thought Doc, if more Guardian Angels listened to their soul we would have more Seniors. There probably could be more Seniors…if only they listened.

"Well, yes, I am a little tired," Doc admitted, answering Michael's question. "It's still a little surreal this promotion and all. I'm sure it will all sink in later tonight."

"When do you officially take over your new One Below?" asked Michael, "I hear it might be a most difficult Seeker."

"Well, my first ten-day Observational period is to take place Monday morning. So, I guess…"

"Monday morning?!" Michael cut in. "Hmph. That's so typical of the Academy. Monday morning indeed. So predictable. So much for out with the old and in with the new, eh? The Academy board of directors keeps saying they're going to modernize and cast off vestiges of the Old Doctrine but it's apparent they're doing the start of Observations just like always—on Monday morning……oh well, to no great mischief, I suppose. I see the conservative wing of the Academy is still thinking inside the box. Huh, same old situation. The progressive wing, wanting change, says 'think outside the box.' Apparently, that's the latest catch phrase up Here and Below—'think outside the box.' Nonsense. I say 'box?…what box?…there's a box?' Both of them got it wrong. Why should anyone have to think inside or outside a box or any shape for that matter? Think on a wide-open plane, I say. It makes for clearer thinking and better thoughts." Michael finished with a satisfying grin. Strange, but conformity and doctrine were not his strong points.

"So, Doc, tell me," Michael said, "…tell me, why do they call you 'Doc'?"

An odd question, thought Doc. But when the Archangel asks, one answers—silly fits or no. "I slipped and fell off a dock into the water Below when I was little. My friends were contemplating calling me Slip, but I guess they liked Doc better. Dock was too long, so they shortened it to Doc," Doc said without cracking a smile. "I've been Doc ever since."

"Oh, I see," Michael said with a hint of disappointment. "Where's the fun in that story? Your chums didn't give you that name because they thought you looked like one of the Seven Dwarves? Or perhaps they thought you were a touch off, maybe like say Dr. Feelgood? Or that you, on occasion, might have resembled Doc Holliday, you know, Wyatt Earp's loveable sidekick forever immortalized by the great Val Kilmer?"

"No, just plain old 'Doc' because I fell. I always seemed to fall and stumble when I was a kid Below......although I did enjoy Mr. Kilmer's work."

"Yes, he was great wasn't he…should've won an Academy Award. Oh well, regardless of your name's origin, I like it," Michael said reassuringly. "Doc is a cool name. I think it's great that our new Senior is Doc. Kind of anti-establishment. Who knows…well, He knows but besides Him…ok, I know…but besides He and I, who knows, maybe you have it in you to be a great Counsel on the Inner Circle? Wouldn't that be just splendid, one of the most famous and great Guardian Angels—Doc. I positively love it. Propensity for stumbling and all. By the way, what was your real name Below?"

"Miiichael," said Doc slowly, but chuckling.

"Ah, yes, I see…well then, Doc will do just fine…."

3

WHITHER WISDOM HIDE?

"So, tell me, *Doc*, how was it being a Basic and Junior?"

"It was great fun—always being there to help in times of need," Doc said. "Rewarding too, knowing that a well-positioned teddy bear just so on the floor could divert attention away from the awaiting danger that beckoned on the top of an open set of stairs. Guarding infants who hadn't yet discovered the feeling of fear as they crawled towards an open set of stairs kept me on my toes for sure. And, as a Junior, watching over the older kids was great fun also. Kids do the funniest things sometimes. Well, funny now that I've had a chance to look back on some of the guarding I've had to do—but I guess it didn't seem so funny at the time."

"Yes, yes, babies and kids will do some strange things sometimes.

Tell me," started Michael, changing the subject "did you ever wonder if your young assignments Below believed in God?"

"No, not really. The thought never crossed my mind," Doc replied as he began to think about Michael's question. "I suppose the infants obviously wouldn't know about God yet and I guess whether an older child or a teenager believed in God would be largely dependant upon their upbringing."

Michael's question made Doc think and prompted one of his own. "But," Doc said as he started his question with a most serious look on his face, "all babies and kids have Guardian Angels don't they, whether they believe in God or not? I mean, God gives each person a Guardian Angel, doesn't He?"

"Well, yes......and then no...maybe."

"Oh, I see. Yes, and then no, and maybe. You're sure?"

"Yes, I'm sure, kind of. Never mind, at least I know what I know and know what I don't know," Michael retorted. He paused. But then how could I know what I don't. His head started to do small circles as if trying to follow his own absurd reasoning. Just as he was getting dizzy, he snapped out of it. "Like I said, never mind......and to get back to your question, I'll begin with the 'yes' part. Yeah, He gives every single person a Guardian Angel when they are born. That's a fact. So, yes, every baby is guarded by one of us. Even as kids grow older they still have a constant companion up Here in a Guardian Angel. However, not everyone will live their entire life with one at their side. So I guess that's the 'no' part."

"How so?" Doc asked, not quite understanding how One Below could be assigned a Guardian Angel at birth and then lose it later on.

"It's like this, my boy," Michael began. "God loves every single person born unconditionally. Because infants and kids don't have the sufficient knowledge to understand such concepts as God, He, through Guardian Angels, or sometimes by Himself, ensures that they are guarded. However, when those people Below are old enough to understand the concept of God and in fact have been exposed to His existence through school, church, friends or what have you, then those people in fact make the decision whether a Guardian Angel will shadow them for the rest of their lives."

"I don't think I quite follow you," Doc said in a low voice, almost ashamed that he was now a Senior and he was still learning something new every day about the guardianship business. He had often wondered why some people as they got older shed—by their own doing—their Guardian Angel.

"Well, it's quite simple really, if you unpack the question and get down to first principles," Michael said kindly, not wanting to shake Doc's confidence. "Once the person Below is old enough to believe or disbelieve in God, then that is when they make the decision on whether they will be accompanied by a Guardian Angel henceforth. If, say, at the age of twenty, that person doesn't believe in God, then that person has no Guardian Angel. Plain and simple. How could it be any other way? Surely, someone can't say they don't believe in God and then relate to their friends that their Guardian Angel helped them in some form or another. No, if a person who doesn't believe in God is somehow helped in a mysterious way, then that was pure coincidence. Coincidences, I might add, run out sooner or later. Guardian Angels, when assigned to a believer will never leave their side as long as they still believe in God. They may never experience Pure Joy, but at least they'll always have a Guardian Angel. Yes, to have a Guardian Angel past the point where the One Below can make a decision about their belief in God, is to tell Him that 'Yes, I believe in You.'"

"So not every adult has a Guardian Angel assigned to them. It depends entirely on whether they believe in God. It's entirely up to them?" Doc asked.

"Correct you are," Michael said with a smile, happy that his new Senior was a quick learner.

"How could it be any other way, really?" posed Michael. "Think of it. How can someone say they don't believe in God in one sentence and in the next sentence affirm their belief in being guarded by a Guardian Angel? Angels, Guardian or otherwise, exist because of God. If the One Below doesn't believe in the Angel's Creator how can they rightly believe in the Angel itself. If it were the other way around, that would be like having your cake and eating it too." At that moment Michael was actually thinking about getting a nice, thick slice of Grandma Johnston's chocolate cake with her secret icing on top. It was common knowledge Above that her chocolate cake was to die for.

"Well, that makes sense," agreed Doc. "So, if a non-believer Below, at some point in later years, changes their mind for whatever reason and comes to believe in God, I assume that a Guardian Angel is then assigned," stated Doc half knowingly, half quizzically.

"Correct you are again," Michael said. "As soon as the One Below believes in the existence of God, then—*presto*—a Guardian Angel is summoned from the Waiting Dock and given their new…excuse me…sorry, uh, mmmm, one moment…assignment."

When Michael said "presto" instantly a piece of chocolate cake was on a plate in his hand and he had it half gone before he finished his sentence.

"Oh, I'm sorry, did you want some?"

"Uh, no thanks." He already had two pieces at the Academy's graduation reception while listening to the congratulatory remarks that were being bestowed on him. "But how did you do that?"

"Tricks of the Inner Circle. Being on His Inner Circle has privileges you know. Stick around for a few hundred years and I might let you in on it."

Doc was thinking about what Michael had said about only people who believe in God when they are old enough to make their own determination as to His existence have the companionship of a Guardian Angel. He was also thinking about the fact that someone could reject God while living Below for fifty years and then all of a sudden embrace His existence and that fact alone would ensure that for the rest of the person's life they would be shadowed by a Guardian Angel.

"I guess," Doc said as he was figuring out the meaning of Michael's premise, "that proves that God really does love His people Below. I mean if someone not only rejects God for years and years and even might do so publicly by voicing their disdain for Him…" he paused as he was finishing his thought as if to get the right words, "…then, if they at some point—after years of hating and disbelieving—believe in His existence, He will forgive their disbelief and immediately send a Guardian Angel to shadow and serve them. Wow! That's love eh, Michael?"

"It sure is," agreed Michael as he wiped the last bit of icing from his chin.

"Funny isn't it," Michael said, as he loosened his sash just a touch, "that many, many people Below don't believe in God—maybe they think it's not 'cool' or something—yet they think that they are guarded by one of us up Here. A preposterous notion really, once you think about it."

While getting most of what Michael said, Doc still had a bit of confusion. "What about when people kind of believe in God and well…maybe kind of don't…like they're not sure. They're sure when they're in times of crisis because they pray to God for help, or when they're at a funeral, and they think that God will surely take care of their departed friend—but besides times like that they shut God out and never think twice about Him. What about that, Michael?"

"Very good question, my lad. Yes, those people who are only believers in times of need have a Guardian Angel……at least they believe. But I can tell you they're probably not guarded by a Senior. Well, at least not a *great* Senior. Well, unless of course God assigns one especially to them. Possible, but rare. No, usually, they have a very capable Junior. Why? Because they really haven't truly bought into God's existence yet. Call them fair-weather-believers-in-times-of-crisis, if you will. Yes, they'll have a Junior assigned and if the Junior is on the ball he will try to subtly convert them into full-time believers. But most part-time believers don't become full-time believers and most Juniors don't convert. Of course, that's only a generalization…if you get my meaning. No, the fact is is that most of the fair-weather believers don't care to believe in earnest. That's ok though, because God will gladly take the fair-weather believers over a non-believer any day. He's not that picky, you know. Very easy to please, He is. A rather pleasurable fellow to deal with too, by the way."

That answered Doc's question.

"But do you know what really makes God smile?" asked Michael.

"What?"

"He smiles most," said Michael, "when someone Below believes in Him and gives thanks to Him when everything is going fine. When their job is fine, their personal relationships are fine and when their finances are fine and they still converse with Him in their own special way or otherwise make it known to Him that they still believe......that's when He is most happy. Because usually it's when things go wrong, as they sometimes will, and the road they're on seems all uphill, that people Below invoke the Almighty. He always hopes that those who believe only in times of crisis will buy into Him on a more full-time basis. He's their friend *all* the time, you know."

"It's funny you say that, Michael, because when I was Below, I always had the feeling," Doc said with a little more self-confidence at conversing with the Archangel, "that your best friend was Someone you never saw, were never introduced to, never met, and never had a face-to-face conversation with and that Person, so to speak, is God. He's everybody's best friend—or could be. All people need do is allow Him to be their friend. He never abandons you. He doesn't ask for much. He certainly doesn't ask for money. He doesn't talk about you behind your back. He never breaks your trust. He will wipe every tear from your eyes. All He asks is that you believe in Him. All He asks from people Below is that you let Him be your friend. That's certainly not much to ask. Yet so many people, for whatever reason, reject His friendship—even His existence—without ever giving Him a chance. And now I know that He even throws in one of us until the end of their days as a bonus if they believe. Am

I right Michael, am I right that He really is each and everyone's greatest friend Below?"

Michael thought to himself that there certainly was a bonus in the deal for whoever Below got Doc. "Yes, Doc, you're right. You see, when you lived Below you must have understood from an early age......," cutting his thought short, Michael asked a new question, "Tell me, exactly what age were you when you believed in God and that He was your best friend?"

"Well, I was very young when I first believed in God Below. As soon as I was old enough to know that this guy named God existed and kind of knew what He was and what He stood for, I believed right away. I had a lot of unanswered questions, but I believed even so. I still have unanswered questions. So, I guess I was in my adolescent years when I knew enough about Him to believe in Him. But," Doc continued, "I really didn't see Him as my best friend until, well, I was probably just into my thirties or so."

"Ok, so you believed in God from an early age, Doc, probably due to your upbringing and surroundings, but you only realized decades later that He was your best friend. Many people Below believe in His existence and to those, Guardian Angels will be assigned. Yet the majority of even the believers, never come to terms with the fact their best friend, the friend who will never let them down—ever—is someone they've never met. And that Someone, as you rightly point out, is God."

Michael was impressed that Doc had figured it out Below when he was barely in his thirties. "That takes faith, my boy—especially the latter, knowing that your best friend on earth was Someone you never met. Indeed, had no concrete proof He even existed. Believing in the existence of God and that He is your best friend—without ever meeting Him—is a hard task for many people. Having faith is no easy matter. Just ask Thomas, one of the Twelve."

Doc now felt as if he was holding his own in the conversation a little better. "I suppose all God asks from someone Below is a chance to be believed in, a chance to be let into their life and then, maybe over time, perhaps with the help of a good Guardian Angel," said Doc with a sly smile, "then maybe over time the One Below will come to recognize that God is their best friend and the love He shows has no equal."

Michael now felt, quite happily, as if he had an equal partner in the dialogue. "For starters, all He really wants is for people Below to believe in His existence and all that He stands for. With time, if the one Below comes to recognize that God is their best friend and that He will never betray them, then great. First things first though, and because faith is a hard subject to master for most, believing in God will do just fine—for now," said Michael who was very, very happy that Doc was getting it. "You're getting it my boy…good for you."

Doc 'got things' because he just listened to his soul; something he did that made him only *seem* smarter than he was. His soul was the one 'getting it.' "Na, I only listen well."

"Who do you listen too?"

"Nobody in particular," Doc said quietly while looking at the ground as he leaned back on the bench and kicked off his flip-flops and moved his feet over the ground. Feeling the cooling and soothing effect, Doc's bare feet loved to mingle with the grass.

"Oh, come on, you must listen to somebody…a favourite professor maybe?"

Doc wasn't sure if he should tell the Archangel that he 'got' most things by listening to his soul.

"Well…who do you listen too?" asked Michael once again coaxing an answer from Doc.

"My soul," Doc said under his breath, afraid that Michael would laugh at him.

Michael raised an eyebrow curiously at Doc. Never before had Michael heard a young Guardian Angel say that. Very impressed with Doc's ability to tap into the wisdom of his soul, he nodded his approval to Doc like a parent subtly affirming the child's successful try at tying their shoe. "I see. Not a bad thing to listen too."

Doc was just glad that the Archangel didn't laugh.

4

PRIMO INTER PARES

Getting back to the conversation at hand, Doc piped in. "Soooo, with the belief in God comes their Guardian Angel and with the Guardian Angel comes...what? I mean, besides traffic diversions and protection and the like?"

"Well, hopefully a safe life, health, luck and so on, and for a very select few—Pure Joy," stated Michael. "But it really depends."

"Onnn......?"

"On lots of things," said Michael who wasn't willing yet to let Doc in on *all* the secrets. "Those things you will no doubt find out in due course...but I'd really like to know what you thought about your time in the Academy studying Senior Theory. Did you enjoy your time there?"

"Well, you learn a lot, that's for sure. And I know more," Doc started.

Michael groaned. No, Doc, please, don't start that again, he thought. Don't start the bit about 'the more I know, the less I know.' My head can't take it. His head started to move in circles again.

"I never realized how little I knew as a Basic and Junior. Senior Theory really takes this guardianship business to a new level. Kind of like the difference between the big leagues and the little leagues. The courses went over a lot of new material, most of which was foreign to me and quite a bit of it I had a hard time understanding the connection between the subject matter and how it had anything to do—if at all—with being a Guardian Angel. So, without rambling on too much—sorry—I did like Senior Theory and I learned an incredible amount......all of which I haven't the foggiest idea how to utilize to better serve my assignment Below. Does that answer your question?"

Doc also wondered why the Academy, when they were teaching him Senior Theory, had not told him that the belief in God was a prerequisite for all adults in order to be assigned a Guardian Angel. That, you would think, thought Doc, would surely have been on the curriculum or in a text.

Out of the blue, Michael spoke. "Not all things you learn come from textbooks, you know. And back to your dilemma, the reason for what you learn in school might not become apparent for some time. But one day you'll go, 'Ohhhh, now I get it.' As good as Professor Christian's book is, it can't contain everything you will need to know as a Senior. Remarkable man, Christian—William that is. He truly cares for his students. And, besides him, many of this term's professors are perhaps the best ever assembled at one time you know: Ewan, Delisle, Clarke, Wright, Eidlin, Torigian, Stratas, Corbett, Toufayan, Fulkerson, Clemons, P.J., Nadon and Woodrow; they're all superb."

Doc nodded his head. He had been taught by each one and each not only was a great teacher but they, in their own way, inspired Doc and instilled in him the will to learn. To learn more. Each one made learning fun, made it cool...there was excitement in it! Too bad more teachers, Below and Above, didn't get it.

Michael continued, "...some of the most important things you learn up Here and some of the most important things you learn during your time Below don't come from institutions of higher learning either you know. Some things you learn by living. Other things you learn by listening. You know, I never learned a whole lot when I was talking," Michael said as he finished with a smile.

"Then I guess," said Doc as it was all sinking in, "it's lucky for me you were sitting here isn't it?"

"I guess it was," answered Michael with a twinkle in his eye. "Everything happens for a reason, I suppose."

"Well, one thing that was part of Senior Theory, that I really don't know why was part of the course, was the part on Economics and Consumption. I still haven't figured that one out quite yet. But I will."

"Economics and Consumption?" repeated Michael.

"Yeah...Economics and Consumption."

"What?! You don't think we Angels have to pay attention to economic patterns, market forces, and consumption trends Below?" asked Michael. "Son," Michael said in an all-knowing manner, "we have to pay attention to *everything*. We would be doing our charges Below a disservice if we didn't pay attention to all that goes on in their life down there. Guarding is more than traffic diversions and chance meetings, you know. Well, they're not 'chance' meetings if we arrange them are they? Actually, I meant *arranged* meetings."

"I know, I know. Guarding is more than traffic diversions and arranged meetings," replied Doc. "It's just I wasn't quite clear on the connection to Economics and Consumption, that's all."

"Would you like me to connect the dots for you?" asked Michael.

"Sure. Well, how about you give me all the dots and see if I can then make the connection myself? I think William left out a few dots in his textbook. No doubt the editor's oversight."

"Mmmm, oh...of course, yes...no doubt an editorial oversight, to be sure…indeed," agreed Michael sarcastically. "Alright, the main thing you have to remember about economics and consum…oh my gosh, would you just look at the time? Doc dude, I gotta go…I'm the moderator in the Machiavelli-Marx debate. I get to pick the topics so I must get going and write out my questions. If you want my prediction, I say it'll be Machiavelli for the win in devastating knockout fashion after about the fifth or sixth question. Marx will be without his brains, Engels, so it won't be much of a debate. In fact, I'm not even sure why he's on the card. Probably because it's 'M' month and they didn't want to put Machiavelli up against Matthew or Mark. Those two know their stuff, eh?" Michael winked.

"Aaaaaanyway my boy, I'll see you in ten days," Michael said as he got up to leave. "It was great chatting with you."

"Ten days?" Doc asked.

"Yes, ten days, why?……oh, I'm sorry, completely slipped my mind. I will be doing your Observational Interviews. As you know, usually the Academy handles all administrative and promotional matters in the Hierarchy, but the Inner Circle convened and it was thought better if one of us handled your Interviews. You don't think the Inner Circle would let the Academy itself Interview our first under-thirty Senior do you?"

Doc was speechless. Proud and impressed. But speechless. And, entirely unsure of what all the fuss about him was. Sure, he might be a Senior under thirty, but to himself he was just the same old Doc. He didn't get all the fuss. Doc got most things, but he really didn't get what the big deal was about him.

"Gabriel couldn't do your Interviews," said Michael. "He's got something big going on Below. Raphael is busy with a new group of Advanced. Uriel wanted to do them but he could only commit to a few Interviews as he has to sit for his new portrait scheduled for unveiling at the gala opening of the renovated Inner Hall and Buonarroti has only so many days open on which he could paint the portrait. Man, that guy is busy up Here. Raguel and Sariel also wanted to but……ah, who's kidding who, I wanted to do your

Interviews all along…so do them I shall. It's nice being *primo inter pares*. Do you know what *primo inte*…."

"First among equals," replied Doc, smiling.

"'First among equals,' that's right. Very good. Gabriel, Raphael and the rest on the Inner Circle like to describe us that way, but let's face it, I'm first and the rest of them are equals with each other," said the Archangel smiling. "But don't tell them I said that…I think it annoys them. Especially Gabriel, he's touchy that way." Michael chuckled.

"Not a word," promised Doc.

"Very well then, *Doc*, see you in ten days after Monday, say, same time, same place? Deal?"

"Deal," Doc replied with a sense of officiousness. "But what do I do? Nobody has told me what I am supposed to do yet."

"Observe."

"Observe what?"

"Observe what you see Below and tell me what you've learned."

"What if I don't learn anything?"

"Then listen. I hear you're good at listening."

And with that, Michael was off to his debate and Doc was left standing at the bench thinking about all that the Archangel had said. His Observational Period didn't start until Monday so he still had a few days with which he could skim his Senior Theory notes for one last final cram. And do some weeding.

As Doc started to walk away, he noticed a piece of discarded scrap paper blowing across the path in the breeze. He immediately picked it up—as it was everybody's duty Above to pick up all garbage on pathways and deposit it in the nearest garbage can. Doc crumpled it up and put it in his pocket and headed for home. It had been a good day. Doc smiled.

5

the HIeRaRCHy

Doc had guardianship over others before, but this new assignment would be different. It would be a greater challenge, this new One Below.

He had proven his capabilities and it was time to move him up—and time for him to learn more. He had just graduated from Phase III at the Academy—the centre for higher learning for Guardian Angels. He was now a Senior Candidate Guardian Angel—the third classification in the hierarchy of Guardian Angels and the second highest, beyond Basic and Junior, and just under Advanced or High as it is sometimes called by the older ones. Technically, he wasn't a full Senior Guardian Angel yet; that would come when he passed his Observational Interviews. However, once Senior Theory is passed, the Guardian Angel is recognized as a *de facto* Senior as the Interviews usually were rubber stamp approvals. But the number of confirmatory Interviews varied between Candidates. Some needed many Interviews; others, less so.

The real learning started when a Guardian Angel became a Senior. Seniors learned—really learned—about God. About His ways. About how things worked Below and Above. They would learn about the philosophy of life, of death, patience, why things happen, why things didn't happen. They would learn about God's Parchment on which the life of the One Below is charted. They would learn about how everything in life is connected. And, most importantly, they would learn how they, as Guardian Angels, fit into His plans for people Below by working with them: as messengers, silent communicators, a shoulder when needed, a guide when called upon—and not just as a protector creating traffic diversions in the name of safety.

To be a Senior was a great honour. To be a Senior successful at guiding their One Below to the pinnacle of their potential was an even greater honour. Success—really true success—was rare. Such success only happened when the One Below and their Guardian Angel were in lockstep—together in mind, together in soul. When that occurred it was widely recognized Above as a true match made in Heaven. The result was Pure Joy.

Doc had been a Basic Guardian Angel for the extremely short time of nine years. From there he spent the unheard amount of time—just seventeen years—as a Junior.

Here he was, his first day as a Senior Candidate Guardian Angel with only twenty-six years in the business. Only twenty-six years! Only twenty-six years to learn his craft. To watch over. To protect. To prod. To suggest. And, most importantly, to learn. The real learning was yet to come though—just as it would be for his new One Below. If a Guardian Angel makes it to be a Senior in under thirty years it's whispered that he's a child prodigy, a genius, one-in-a-million. Of course, Doc never saw himself as a genius. He just saw himself as an ordinary, average guy, who at some point in his life Below worked hard and listened to his soul. Above, he did exactly the same. Odd, but Doc wasn't a genius; the only thing he did differently than most people was listen to his soul. More odd was the fact that when Doc listened...his soul always spoke to him. Every soul speaks. Not every soul is heard. Doc's genius was in listening to his soul. Simplistic genius.

Though still years off, Doc was a sure bet—the consensus held—for the Guardian Angel Hall of Fame after he completed his final guardianship as an Advanced Guardian Angel.

After Advanced, and in addition to his induction into the Hall, he would be almost certain to attain the seldom awarded title of Counsel. As Counsel, he would be eligible to put in for a professorship at the Academy to teach up-and-coming Guardian Angels. But gaining one of the fifty rotating professorships was the stuff of politics and perhaps, as viewed by some, a superfluous appointment. Though it is true, the Academy *did* have some outstanding instructors who merited a professorship regardless of the politicalities of the appointment.

What wasn't superfluous was the even less awarded seat on The Inner Circle: the most prestigious of heavenly, angelic bodies. Only the greatest of Angels were named to this group of wise counsel. If a decision of any importance had to be made in Heaven that didn't need God's direct involvement, it lay with The Inner Circle. Some thought that Doc would eventually be named to The Inner Circle; an endorsement that must come from God. Being on The Inner Circle was a lifelong position, that is, forever. Less than ten Guardian Angels sit as Counsel on The Inner Circle.

With his new assignment Doc really would be a true Senior. Entrusted to be Guardian Angel over a charge Below that would test his true mettle, his level of patience and his true level of knowledge. If together in soul, the success would be Pure Joy.

Gone were his old charges that he had guardianship over as a Basic and Junior. Gone was a young girl Below of ten years of age who had a propensity for not looking both ways when she crossed the street. Doc was busy with her. Always having to make sure her book-bag strap got caught on a signpost or the like just before she hastily and absent-mindedly ran out into traffic. Or, in some instances, he would throw up a quick red light on a set of traffic lights instead of allowing the anticipated longer green.

Important stuff that—playing with traffic. Important stuff that any Guardian Angel worth their salt had to be adept at. Mundane, yes, but necessary for any Guardian Angel to have in their repertoire. Necessary indeed. Rewarding too.

Doc learned, and then used, over eighty different ways to play with traffic while he was a Basic and by the time he was a Junior he had over 100 so-called traffic diversions at the ready to be employed at any given time. That fact, the fact that he had over 100 traffic diversionary tactics, was amazing. No…unheard of.

The texts at the Academy said that each Basic Guardian Angel should learn between forty and fifty of the ninety known ways to alter traffic patterns so as to be able to serve their One Below with the highest competence. As a Junior and upward, it was expected that one would learn all ninety ways to play with traffic while attending to the One Below if needed. Doc just didn't learn the ninety, he strived until he came up with more. Doc had over 100. Not even an Advanced Guardian Angel had surpassed the century mark. Doc was a striver.

There were other youngsters who were under Doc's guardianship when he was a Basic and Junior besides his forgetful little girl. He taught some, guided others. He was not content with just guarding, a fact that did not slip the notice of the Academy. But the majority of his detail usually boiled down to just guarding, because, that's what most Guardian Angels do—guard.

Not all Guardian Angels reach the rank of Senior or Advanced where they are less occupied with guarding and more involved with communicating, guiding and teaching. Just like some people Below, some Guardian Angels attain their potential; some do not.

It is said that a Basic Guardian Angel is anything but. In fact, as it has been argued, Basic Guardian Angels have the most important task of all the ranks in the Guardian Angel Hierarchy. It was true that when Angels entered the ranks of Guardian Angels and thus embarked on the guardianship business they had no previous guarding experience, but their task, while extremely important, was rather easy in that it didn't require much experience.

These Basic, newly-minted Guardian Angels had really only one job description: to guard and protect. Each new Basic Guardian Angel is given the task of protecting a newborn Below. Every infant Below born of all countries, races, nationalities, religions—it matters not—receives a Basic Guardian Angel.

The new Guardian Angel need not teach, nor communicate. No guiding, no converting to do. God, God's existence, or His plan for the infant in later years, never entered into the picture. Just guarding and protecting. Making sure toddlers didn't choke on their first bites of solid food before they got the hang of it. Making sure they didn't stop breathing in their sleep if they rolled the wrong way. Making sure the crazy crawlers didn't crawl, or rather, tumble down two flights of stairs.

More often than not, the fit is perfect. A new toddler keen to explore is matched with a new Basic Guardian Angel—with no previous practical experience—keen to guard. Easy stuff for the Guardian Angel. Protection and vigilance. That was the name of the game. The only thing a newborn is concerned with is survival and the Basic Guardian Angel's job was to see to it.

A Junior Guardian Angel, one step up in the Hierarchy, had slightly more responsibilities than a Basic. However, the main task of a Junior was still to guard and protect. Juniors, by far, outnumbered all the ranks combined. While Basic Guardian Angels were, for the most part, concerned with infants, Juniors on the other hand looked after Ones Below in all age categories.

Juniors had carriage over all children, excluding infants, and all adolescents. Almost all teenagers had a Junior guarding them. And, the majority of adults were guarded by Juniors.

Their main task was still to protect and guard. Occasionally, Juniors would guide and teach their charge Below, but seldom. There was not usually the need to. Juniors were numerous—the most numerous class.

Adults Below, that live day in and day out without thinking, challenging, seeking or striving, were numerous. Indeed, they were the most numerous class Below. Juniors had charge of these people Below—those that were just living their lives by going through the motions. They cared little for changing their lot in life—happy or not.

Children and adolescents were busy with friends, school, sports and scraped knees. They were not yet concerned so much with life and the path on which they would live it. Juniors could look after them just fine.

Teenagers were concerned about proving their parents wrong and with growing pains. They weren't delving into life with deep thought or capable of charting their course. Juniors could look after them just fine too.

And, the majority of adults who were guarded by Juniors were concerned with going to work, coming home, being happy—or not. The happy part, like every other aspect of their life, was truly up to them. The majority of adults have the ability to strive and seek yet did nothing of the sort. Their lives were on cruise control—for better or for worse—and they weren't really interested in learning, striving and questioning.

From an early age, perhaps shortly after their teens, most adults relegated themselves to the fact that the course their life was on at the present was the course that they were going to stay on. Happy or not. It's where they were and they had not the energy, ambition nor desire to change it. Yes, the majority of adults content with cruise control had no use for a Senior Guardian Angel—a Guardian Angel who would not only guard and protect, but one who would teach, listen, communicate and bring Pure Joy. It is open to all adults to change the course of their lives should they choose—but most didn't.

Because most adults Below couldn't be bothered with seeking or striving they had no use for a great Senior Guardian Angel. Or a Guardian Angel who would become great in time, just as the One Below could become great in time. Posting a Senior to someone Below who lived life by going through the motions would be a waste of precious resources. Juniors were well equipped to deal with the guarding and protecting that the majority of people Below would need in their lifetime.

When those Below decided to seek, to strive in their life—a Senior was commissioned immediately to travel the journey with them. Good Seniors were underused.

Doc blistered through the ranks of Basic and Junior. Before long, as a Basic, he was rolling out garbage cans onto streets—all in the name of safety and guardianship—in his sleep. Unlike many Juniors, he guided some teenagers away from crime and hate. He just didn't guard and protect; he communicated, taught, strove and learned something new every day.

The Academy saw this. They had to move him up. His obvious talent was not being maximized. Doc's real talent ready to be tapped, the Academy thought—and it was only a hunch at this point—was that of the art of unspoken communication he would share with his One Below. That, was the mark of a great Senior; a great Guardian Angel. If honed properly and used properly, its employ would bring success of epic proportion to both the One Below and the Guardian Angel Above. The Academy had to take the chance. He was ready.

So it was decided to summon Doc for his final Junior exit exams. Upon successful completion—a sure thing—he would spend six months in Senior Theory at the Academy preparing for his Senior entrance exams. Then if passed, Doc, as a newly-minted Senior, the one-in-a-million Guardian Angel, would be ready for his most difficult assignment yet. Everybody, including the Academy and Michael saw Doc as a prodigy; Doc just saw himself as plain, old

Doc. Because of Doc's unquestioned abilities it was rumoured that Doc might receive a Seeker.

Senior Theory exposed the Guardian Angel to new concepts. What the new theory *didn't* do was explain how those concepts were to be intertwined in their work and how they would affect their One Below. That would be done through trial and error. Just like how life is lived Below. Passing Senior exams gave the Guardian Angel more knowledge about the concepts needed to successfully guide their One Below. The practicalities and decisions on when to put those concepts into use were up to the Senior. Ultimately, however, the success of those concepts, when implemented by the Guardian Angel, was mostly up to the One Below. That's why success—real success—was just as dependent upon the One Below as it was on the Guardian Angel. Each had to understand their own part. If they did, the limits of the One Below would be boundless.

Subsequent to passing the Senior Theory entrance exams numerous Observational Periods were scheduled. This was where the new Senior observed life Below—on a general level. The Senior had unfettered access to all Below, unlike their time as Basic or Junior level Guardian Angels when they were solely concerned with the person they were assigned to guard.

The Senior Observational Periods would give the new Senior a chance to view a great many people Below in a variety of situations. After each Observational Period, the Guardian Angel returned to the Academy or to the appointed Instructor to report what they had observed and how they thought they could guide, teach, prod and suggest—and of course, it went without saying, to guard and protect. A given, the task of guarding to a Senior was child's play. However, new work was at hand. Guiding and teaching was the real work of Seniors. A most difficult task! How the new Senior would guide and teach was up to them. Concepts learned in Senior Theory were meant to help them find their way in guiding and teaching their One Below—a way heretofore mostly unknown to them.

The number of Observational Periods each new Senior had to

undergo varied. Sometimes the Academy needed few Observational Periods in which to assess the likelihood of future success of the new Senior. For some, however, many Observational Periods had to be undertaken. No new Senior Candidate was given full Senior status with less than seven Observational Periods and subsequent Interviews. Many thought Doc could do it in five or six.

6

---

existers

First thing Monday morning Doc went about his observing. His first Senior Observational Period had finally arrived.

Because as a Basic and Junior he was accustomed to watching over only one person Below at any given time, Doc decided to first observe a family. More going on, he thought. More learning.

The family he chose as his first Observation case study was an average, typical family of four. The two parents had good jobs; their combined income, decent. Both jobs, though, were not quite what the parents wanted, nor dreamed about in their younger days. But decent and tolerable nonetheless. Their two children, a boy and girl, were five and seven respectively. The family lived in the suburbs of a major city. Everybody seemed generally happy—on the outside.

When Doc peered in for a closer look he was fascinated. This family had everything. Two brand new vehicles sat in the driveway. All the latest home electronic gadgets abounded. The furniture was new and pristine as was everything else in the home. This family lived like it had the household income double of what it really was. This family never did without.

That night Doc paid special attention to a particular conversation between the husband and wife.

"Honey," said the wife, "I was thinking, I think I might leave my job and take those art courses that I've always wanted to take. I only need two more terms at school to finish my fine arts degree. When I attended university just before we got married, my professors all were of the view that I had a great career ahead of me as a professional artist. They saw it in my early work. You know it's something that I've wanted to do for some time now and it's been over ten years since I left my degree in mid-stream. What do you think?"

"I wish you could," replied the husband, "but you know we can't afford it. We need both our incomes to pay our bills. Our mortgage is massive…both entertainment systems were bought without putting any money down and those payments start next month…our bedroom furniture is only about half paid off…and that new flat screen T.V. we decided to buy last month has payments due on it at the start of the new year for three years. That's not counting our utility bill, our two phone bills for each of our cell phones…and besides, we're still paying off our line of credit that was maxed out to pay for our wedding and honeymoon. I'm sorry…we just can't afford it. Besides, my union boss says we might be going on strike next month. If that happens and you left your job, then we wouldn't have *any* income."

"But you don't understand," the wife said firmly, "I…really… hate…my…job. I can't stand it anymore! It's awful. I was never meant to do that for the rest of my life. I was meant to be an artist. I know it."

"Well, you should've thought about that before…" said the husband before he was cut off by his increasingly upset wife.

"'I should have thought of that before…'—is that what you said?" asked the wife bluntly.

"Yes…you should have thought of that before… We just can't afford to have either of us leave our jobs right now. I'm not necessarily thrilled with my job either, you know. You really don't know what it's like to work in that factory do you? I would love to set up that business I've been talking about for five years…I know that's what my calling was. But we're in debt too deeply right now and I doubt that we'll ever be in a position to go after our dreams. Besides, we never do without. Whatever we want, we buy—whether it comes from debt or not. That's not too bad, is it?"

"Yes, it's bad…because our debt is keeping both of us from doing what we *really* want to do," sobbed the wife. She left the kitchen crying. The husband sat there without saying a word.

Doc was astounded. Such a shame. Two people who had everything and never did without were mired in so much debt that it prevented them from following their dreams of doing something else. Debt was stifling their creative passion. It was keeping down their ability to follow their inner desires. To be happy. Both were very, very unhappy people. How could they let it get so far, he asked himself?

Doc never saw things like this as a Basic or Junior and he wondered how common this problem was. He decided to find out. His observations were disappointing and disturbing. Crippling debt was everywhere. People everywhere couldn't follow their dreams because of money…or lack thereof.

Money! Doc yelled to himself silently. How can money control someone's life, especially when they really don't have a shortage of it?!

Doc continued to look. Maybe his first few encounters were anomalous. But after checking with a wide cross-section of many people in both cities and towns, Doc became truly disheartened.

Singles, married couples, teenagers, families—each segment of society was affected by it. Obviously, not *every* person was mired in debt to such an extent that it prevented them from seeking out their dreams and destiny, but a great number were.

Even still, thought Doc, that number is far too high. I can see that a few people would be in over their heads financially—some by their own doing, some by no fault of their own. But many are carrying huge debt loads of their own doing. So many people in today's day and age just never do without! They are being controlled by money, banks and credit card companies. I can't really blame the companies, Doc thought, after all, no one is forcing people to live beyond their means. Even so, Doc felt for their plight.

In the middle of his Observational Period, Doc went home one night and took out his Senior Theory notes and texts on Economics and Consumption. One text said that in some instances a *surplus* of money keeps Ones Below down and conversely, but in the same manner, *lack of* money also keeps people down. He never understood how money—or surplus of money—could stifle someone's destiny. But now he knew.

He now had learned that knowing what to do with one's disposable money is an important decision to make. When he lived Below he was always a patient and conscientious spender. Back then he never realized the sorrow that debt inflicted on the average person. Now he understood that having a comfortable amount of money—short of independent wealth—can be dangerous to the unaware.

With a surplus of money, people Below can buy far more things than they really can afford, thought Doc. When they start living beyond their means they're stuck. I mean really stuck. Keeping up with the neighbours can be devastating. Geesh.

Doc was amazed that all sorts of—and indeed many—people were stuck in life. And also stuck was their ability to do something that made them happy—to create, to think, to question, to believe, to strive, to seek.

All they can do, he thought, is go to the same job that they only tolerate because it provides them with just—sometimes not even—enough money to pay the bills. They're floundering. Mired in debt, they resign themselves to the fact that this will be their lot in life. All they do is exist. That's it! They're Existers. Many are unhappy and many conceivably would want to change the course of their life if they could. They'll never get ahead, Doc said to himself as he skimmed the pages of his text. They're beholden to their debt—the 800 channel t.v., their brand new cars, their gadgets…their…their stuff. Doc started to hate stuff.

What a shame, Doc murmured to himself—they can't explore, discover, learn. The Seeker in them—if it's there at all—won't have a chance to get out. They've resigned themselves to be Existers. Stuff is stifling those who may want to change their life and become a Seeker.

He wasn't quite sure what a Seeker was because neither the texts nor Michael had really spelled it out. But he was sure that a Seeker always looked to do better; to improve, to learn. Perhaps they followed their dreams and goals.

But all these purchases—most of them little things like cell phone bills, monthly cable bills for 100 channels, gadgets they didn't need, stuff that when added up was the main drain on people's resources—reminded Doc of something he heard in Senior Theory.

I think the professor was lecturing on Socrates…no, Aristotle… wait, maybe Plato, ah whatever. Doc shook his head as he tried to recall who exactly the dead white guy was that the professor was talking about.

Yes, I think it was probably Aristotle who said it wasn't so much the huge one-time expenditures that were a drain on one's resources as it was the continuous *little* expenditures that would prove to be the biggest drain. Stuff.

What Doc kept shaking his head in disbelief about was that the reason for all this stifling debt wasn't the lack of money—but rather a surplus of money. People Below had money to buy stuff, so they did. And then, only when they didn't have the money to buy more stuff, they just put it on credit. They could get credit because they had jobs. Barely tolerable jobs. Barely tolerable jobs that they would have to tolerate for at least another five years so they could make the money to pay for the stuff they bought on credit. They bought into deals where they wouldn't have to pay for their purchase for another two years. Then they would buy more stuff that would be paid for by money earned at their barely tolerable job. Then the cycle would start all over again. What an awful cycle, thought Doc. People's life cycle was being dominated by the stuff cycle.

That night at home, Doc was trying to figure out how he, as a Guardian Angel, played a part in all of this. That figuring was troubling.

How in the heavens, can I do anything to help those, who, by their own doing, get caught in debt and thereby might never know what their true calling was? How can I help them think about their folly; how can I help them learn, question, strive, seek? I'm a Guardian Angel, not Oprah!

His brain was saturated with Senior Theory economics and his observations Below. He flipped to other notes and other chapters in the texts: patience, the art of unspoken communication, temptation, classifications of Ones Below, revolving doors, another chapter on patience, yet another on the art of unspoken communication, Temporary Apparent Non-Association Human Intervention or TANAHI for short, things happen for a reason…and the list went on and on. Doc's eyes were starting to close.

"TA-na-hee," pronounced Doc silently and phonetically just before he drifted off. Great, he thought, I can't wait until Michael grills me on *that* subject. I still can't figure out how I can help the folks in debt, let alone the importance of a concept the name of which sounds like…

Exhausted, Doc fell asleep mid-thought.

7

tHe stuff cycLe

When Doc's next waking moment arrived, it was daylight. That day, without figuring out his part in all of this yet, Doc went back to observing.

Not really sure where he would begin, he finally settled— because of a nagging mystery—on going back to one of the same places that he observed the previous night. While observing one family he noticed a huge T.V. that took up half the wall space in which it was placed in front of. What on earth, Doc asked himself previously, is it that people are watching that they need a five-foot T.V. screen? This electronic piece of stuff piqued his curiosity, not only because of its size, but because almost every house he observed had huge televisions—some bigger than others—and they were usually on. Sometimes families had *four or five* televisions.

So, Doc decided to find out for himself what many people Below thought was of such a pressing matter that they had to have huge televisions to watch whatever so often.

Must be really important things that are being shown on T.V. these days, I guess.

Doc observed one house. And another. He observed a tavern and saw what was being watched there. He observed apartments, hospitals, dorm rooms, and then went back and observed more family houses. He realized that everybody had become addicted to television. And, by the end of his sampling, Doc realized that a great portion of the citizenry was addicted to something called "reality T.V." Reality T.V.? Why, it's anything but. It's scripted...it's...it's mindless consumption is what it is. Doc shook his head in disbelief.

Doc went back the next night to see if anything had changed. Each night, he noticed millions upon millions of people were watching "reality T.V." *That* was the pressing matter. The next night he went back again. Every night, night in and night out, these people were addicted to their T.V. screens and especially to reality T.V. shows. He surmised that the same pattern would happen week after week. Month after month. He guessed it could go on year after year.

Doc felt a sense of pity for the people who lived their life watching someone else on a box.

Can they not see? Can they not see that they were wasting their lives?

Doc was miffed. These people were spending precious hours wasting their lives and they not only seemed oblivious to it—they didn't seem to care.

He couldn't help remembering a day earlier that a man Below started to get upset when he had to wait three minutes for his coffee at a drive-thru coffee shop and then became exasperated when he had to wait thirty seconds for an unexpected red light. A little girl crossing the street barely caught his attention as his attention barely caught the red light first. He was a busy man, this rushed driver.

Yet Doc saw that same man that same night watch three consecutive hours of mindless television under the guise of reality—*willingly*. Suddenly Doc made a connection.

These mindless consumers are Existers—just like the mindless spenders, he said to himself. They just barely exist due to the fact that they were born. They don't think, don't challenge, don't strive, don't seek. Their lives are beholden to a talking box. Their reality T.V. addiction is stifling their creativity, their learning…only this time there was no debt keeping them from doing so, although I'll bet some are neck deep in both. They are *voluntarily* allowing the T.V.—and other stuff—to stifle them, to deny their personal destiny. Maybe this activity was their reason for being born. So they could waste life watching reality stuff. *Stuff.*

Doc was beginning to hate that word.

Doc started to debate the mindless consumers in his mind.

Think of the things you could accomplish, if you spent the same amount of time pursuing some interest—a hobby, part-time school, charity work, a part-time job to help pay for the debt that you'll have when you have to pay for that T.V. starting next year. Instead of watching *Survivor City* or *Switching Housewives* you could take guitar lessons or teach yourself to play the guitar. You could write songs… become a successful musician. You could write a book. Take acting lessons. Get a part in the town play. Get noticed by a talent scout. Become a professional actor. Then be a host of your *own* reality T.V. show for goodness sake! But wasting time on myspacebook.com that you'll never get back, just to see pictures of the buddy you see every day anyway…please!!

Doc kept his internal debate going.

Let your mind explore by letting it read a book. It will thank you. Read a book on music, history, a foreign culture…ANYTHING! Don't be a mindless consumer. You're voluntarily wasting your life, yet you yell at someone for not bringing your coffee two minutes sooner. You don't get it do you?

Doc tired himself out debating with thoughts that didn't seem to care one iota. He went back home and got some sleep.

The rest of his first Observational Period was spent looking at more habits of many people Below: over-spending, mindless consumption, blaming others for their woes, stuff. Doc never realized how many people Below voluntarily lived their life in such a way that they themselves were stifling happiness, creativity, denying personal goals, giving up on dreams, forsaking life-long learning and never thinking about striving or seeking.

There's got to be a way to nudge these people out of the static state they're in, thought Doc. They're all on cruise control.

Disheartened and still entirely confused about how he, as a Guardian Angel, could suggest new avenues to these people Below, Doc crawled into bed after his last night of observing. He knew that tomorrow he would have to meet the Archangel and not only explain what he observed but how he would fit into all of this. If his new assignment was One Below who was mired in debt and a voluntary mindless consumer, Doc didn't have a clue how to go about changing him—or at least helping to change him. He slowly started to fall asleep.

Just before he drifted off, Doc bolted upright. "Wait a minute!" he said out loud to his empty bedroom. "I've been given a Seeker, or at least that's who I'm *supposed* to be getting. Surely a Seeker is someone who doesn't spend or consume mindlessly to such an extent that their whole life is dominated by it? I won't have to worry about all this nonsense and stuff. Although, I really don't know what a Seeker is and Michael never told me. What is a Seeker?"

He had an answer, albeit not a great one. A Seeker, Doc told himself, addressing his question for the second time, is someone who is looking to better themselves, who really believes in God, who doesn't buy into all this mindless consumption and is someone who doesn't let stuff control their life. I bet Seekers don't get caught in the Stuff Cycle.

That prompted a new question.

If Seekers don't let stuff control their lives and they keep striving to learn and expand their minds, why do they need me? Why do they need a Guardian Angel? It's the others that seem to be more in need of our services. Well, maybe not. After all, God does help those who help themselves. Maybe, Seekers get Seniors because they've moved beyond just existing and they're busy chasing dreams and destinies. And the road to destinies is a hard road to take—so the services of a good Guardian Angel might come in handy. Maybe that's why Seekers get Seniors—because they're on a tough road.

This had Doc perplexed. He slept on that thought as well.

8

patience

With no sign of Michael, Doc sat down on their bench waiting for the Archangel's arrival. Waiting and thinking. And listening.

Good thing he's not here yet, because I still haven't figured out how the heck I can help the people who seem to be stagnant and floundering in their life. Maybe that's just the way they're supposed to be. Content with being debt-ridden and beholden to mindless consumption.

But something inside him really doubted it. He started to argue with himself.

I suppose, there's nothing I can do if that's the way people *want* to live their lives. It's up to them to change. But there's got to be something more. I'm just not sure what it is. I know Michael will want to know my solution. Maybe he'll let me off the hook…surely he'll be happy with just the fact that I've observed that some people are denying themselves their true destiny in life by their own doing. After all, on the surface it just looks like people are mindless consumers and debt-ridden. It's not everyone, Doc thought—in order to reassure himself—that makes the connection with that fact and the fact that this behaviour is stifling their dreams and goals.

Doc waited some more for Michael to show up. Michael was late, but not that late yet.

After all, we didn't set an exact time—just "same time, same place."

Ten minutes turned into fifteen minutes; fifteen turned into twenty. "Good thing I'm patient," Doc said aloud. "Patience! Patience, is the answer," said Doc a little louder. He looked around to see if anyone heard his outburst. No one was around—not even Michael.

Why, of course, that's it, Doc said to himself as he resumed his silent thoughts. Patience is the answer. If somehow, as a Guardian Angel, I could instill a sense of patience in those people Below, then they might not be so adept at finding themselves in debt. Restraint, that's the key. If some of these people showed restraint when it came to buying stuff that they really didn't need nor could afford then maybe some of them would be in a position to—because they're no longer in debt and chained to a barely tolerable job—change the course of their life.

Obviously, he thought to himself as he continued to work on his premise, that would be up to the people Below. Because, after all, they are masters of their own destiny. True, it would take some time, but that's all these people Below have is time. It might take three to five years to get out of debt—along with some discipline—but they're probably going to live for another forty or fifty years. What's five years out of fifty?

If only more people Below used and experienced short-term pain for long-term gain. Why, that wife I observed, thought Doc, could, after a few years, take those art courses. She could become the artist that she always wanted to be. It would take some time and hard work at showing continuous restraint, but she could do it if she wanted to—I know she could.

Doc knew the old saying, 'You made your bed and now you have to lie in it,' but figured that there was nothing preventing a person from getting up and making it again.

Feeling a little better at figuring it out in his mind, Doc now knew what he would tell Michael on his arrival. He still hadn't figured out *how* to help these people—regardless of their predicament—but he was feeling good about how he had figured out that patience could help some people Below show some restraint in their lives and thereby maybe realize their personal goals.

But how do I do that—teach patience?

He continued thinking.

I have to intervene, somehow. Like, intervene in a physical way or something. Teaching patience or guiding in general is not the same thing as rolling out garbage cans into traffic. Making someone change their ways—if they're open to the idea—is more than protecting. How the heck do I teach patience if I can't talk to them…if I can't communicate with them?

"Waait a minute," Doc said aloud. "Communication. Michael spoke of it and it was a subject in Senior Theory. That must be it…I have to communicate with my assignment Below. How will I make them listen to me? But how do I do that if I can't go down and talk with them?" That was Doc's new problem.

9

tHe ROCk staR

Doc kept looking for Michael, proud that he thought of a way that he could potentially help these people Below, but a little frustrated that he had not yet figured how to go about it. He kept waiting for Michael.

"Good thing I'm patient eh?" he said aloud to a chipmunk, who seemed anything but, and seemed oblivious to Doc's presence as it scampered along on the grass in front of Doc who was now firmly planted on the bench waiting for the Archangel. He wondered if it was Edmund...he couldn't tell one chipmunk from the next.

Doc didn't know it, but it was Edmund. Where there's Edmund, the Archangel is not far off. Not a moment after he finished outlining to himself what he would tell Michael, along came the

Archangel from some distance down the path.

As Michael got closer, Doc noticed the Archangel was waving his arms in up and down motions and at different intervals. Sometimes it looked as though he was hitting an imaginary object in front of him, then off to the side, then at eye level off to the right and left. His legs were moving in contorted rhythms—not quite walking, nor running, nor dancing nor jumping. Now he looked as if he was holding something in front of him with has hands, which he was moving furiously from side to side and up and down. His body was moving from side to side. Doc could also see that Michael had really let his hair down today and it was going all over the place as his head was bouncing up and down.

Doc thought Michael was being chased by wasps or something. However, as Michael got closer Doc could see no swarms or singles. Michael wasn't yelling or shouting or otherwise making any noises denoting distress.

As Michael got within speaking distance, Doc said hello.

"Hey Michael, what's up?" asked Doc politely. The Archangel didn't answer. Not wanting to ask Michael outright what he was doing, but still curious as to what was going on, Doc spoke again.

"How are things Michael…you doing alright?" He asked the question nonchalantly as he was now becoming increasingly more at ease talking with the Archangel.

Michael stopped his performance just as he approached Doc. "Sorry, what did you say? I couldn't hear you," Michael said. Doc thought that strange as Michael was only about fifteen feet from him when he said hello. "Oh nothing really," said Doc, "I just asked if you were alright."

"Me? I'm fine, why? Why am I not fine?"

"Well, it's just that when you were waving your arms and such. I thought you were maybe being chased by bees or something…or maybe wasps. They can be nasty sometimes."

"Waving my arms? I was? A WASP?" asked Michael. "No, I really don't like their music. They're too weird for me…the band WASP that is. No, I was listening to Metallica, one of the greatest heavy metal bands of all time. Man, are they great. I was listening to them just now in my head—full volume—and I was playing along with them. I think you saw me as I was playing along to 'Wherever I May Roam.' What a great tune! They have so many great tunes."

Metallica? Wherever I May Roam? Doc said to himself.

"Metallica? Wherever I May Roam?" Doc repeated aloud. "Is that what you were doing…I mean playing…er, listening too," said Doc as he looked around for a headset or some kind of portable audio system. There was none.

"Yeah, that's right," replied Michael curtly. "What's wrong with that? Is that ok?"

"Uh…sure, of course, whatever does it for you, I guess," Doc said, still in a state of mild shock after learning that the Archangel, he who is like God, listens to Metallica.

"The guys in Metallica," Michael started, "are all great—every single one of them. They are, quite simply…awesome. You heard of them?"

"Yup."

"Like 'em?"

"Actually, yeah, I do. But GnR are good also. And I'm not convinced that there's been a greater band than Pearl Jam. Pearl Jam might be the best of all time. The Crue aren't bad either too, you know?"

"The Crue? As in Motley Crue? Yup, they pretty much rock. Their front man, Vince Neil—he pretty much has a voice that's outta this world. Not quite up to Eddie Vedder's baritone, but spectacular all the same. Remind me to introduce you to Vince's Guardian Angel sometime. Fellow bandmate Nikki Sixx has one of the best guarding him too. Lord knows he needs it. Come to think of it, they all have been keeping their Guardian Angels pretty busy. Now, Vince, there's a guy who's had some ups and downs, but over time he's overcome some big obstacles. Kind of a striver, if you will. But back to the boys in Metallica though—what's your favourite Metallica song?"

"Hmmm, I'm not sure.....'Wherever I May Roam' is good," Doc replied as he tried to remember more Metallica songs, "but I also like 'No Leaf Clover' and some of their early stuff is good too...I don't know which one is my favourite, they have so many."

Michael's eyes lit up with excitement. "You like 'No Leaf Clover' too? No way! That's wicked! That song is amaaazing...Dun da da Dun da da Dun da da Dun DAA...Dun da da Dun da da Dun da da Dun DAA...Dun da da Dun da da Dun da da Dun DAA...Dun DAA...Dun DAA...DUN," Michael sounded out as if he was playing guitar, bass and drums simultaneously in front of a full stadium of fans. "Those dudes can rock, eh?"

"Sure can," agreed Doc. For some reason he immediately thought that at some point the guys in that band started out playing instruments as kids and then just kept at, worked hard and then, over time, became planetary rock stars. Their reach was international, global...truly planetary. Other kids could do that too, he thought. If only more kids could peel themselves away from the t.v. and pick up a guitar and dream about playing in front of 50,000 people at an outdoor festival...their dreams could come true too. Metallica or Motley Crue or U2 or Pearl Jam, he thought, didn't become superstars in one year. They worked hard and reached their destiny. They strove to be the best. Doc admired that. Apparently, so did Michael.

10

DEath aND GRaNDMothERS

Setting aside his rock star alter ego, Michael got down to business at hand. "So, how was your first Observational Period?"

"It was fine. Well, fine in the sense that it went along ok without any hitches and I guess fine insofar that I was able to observe lots of…well, actually…no Michael, it didn't go fine."

"What do you mean, it didn't go fine? You didn't get hurt did you? You didn't go down there did you? Oh no, you went Below didn't you? You can't dooo that…it's not allowed. Well, not really. I mean…never mind, we'll get into that later. Tell me you didn't go down Below?"

"Don't worry…I didn't go Below. That's the first thing they teach you in Basic…never go down Below." Hearing Michael say that going Below "is not allowed…well, not really," had Doc wondering. However, for the moment, he decided to leave it.

"Ok, what didn't go fine then?" asked Michael.

"Well, for starters, there are a lot of people Below in crippling debt. Many people. And there are many people Below who are very adept at—experts, if you will—mindless consumption."

"Yeah…go on."

"For instance…debt. It's everywhere," Doc said as he was remembering what he had observed Below in all cross-sections of life at almost epidemic proportions. "And not just debt carried over from one weekly paycheque to the next. The debt I observed was pervasive. Now, I only had ten days to figure out what it all meant, but I would suggest that this debt load that many people down Below are carrying is being carried not only week to week—which I observed first hand—but because of the amount of it that individuals and families carried, I would say that it carries on from month to month and, in most cases, year to year. It touched all types of people from singles to families to couples. Obviously, there were plenty of people who weren't in debt, but…I don't know…it just seemed that far too many ordinary people with disposable money were finding themselves in debt. Only, I guess they weren't *finding* themselves in debt, as it were, but they were rather taking themselves there…knowingly. Pity, really."

Before he spoke, Michael silently agreed with Doc's last statement. People don't just happen to find themselves in debt one day; no, they know full well where they are going and consent to going there all on their own.

"So," replied Michael, wanting to hear Doc's argument.

"So?!" said Doc with disbelief.

"Yeah…so what? Maybe they like being in debt. Did you ever think of that? Maybe they like never having to do without—whether it comes by way of overspending or not."

"I doubt it," said Doc.

"Why do you doubt it?"

"Because it was keeping some of the people down."

"What do you mean, keeping people down?"

"Well, in one family, the wife wanted to follow her dream of being an artist. She hated her job and she wanted to break free and follow her desires, follow the path her heart had always hoped she'd take one day. The upshot is, she can't. She desperately wants to, but her family is so heavily in debt because of 'stuff' that she quite literally can't afford to quit her job and follow her dreams. That's what I mean when I say that sometimes debt has the effect of keeping people down. It is stifling their true calling. Debt was stifling her husband too."

"Well then," Michael chimed in, "maybe her true calling was to be in debt and have lots of stuff and never having to do without. Maybe that's her destiny. Maybe it's her husband's destiny too."

"How can you say that, Michael?" Doc said, becoming quite annoyed with Michael's solution.

True, Doc thought it also, but he didn't believe it. "How can you say *that* is her destiny in life, when I heard her saying she hated her job and she wanted to do something else? Being an artist was to be her destiny, not being mired in debt and stuff."

"Yes, but until she—or anybody else for that matter—changes their ways then it will be their destiny to live the way they currently do," Michael offered. "People Below—in their life, job, relationships, finances and the like—are exactly where they are supposed to be at that moment. *Exactly.* It's like a snapshot capturing space and time. Right at that moment—right when you observed all these people—you saw them exactly at the spot where they're supposed to be. Oh sure, some people experience negative things not of their doing and you kind of have to feel sorry for them for that—but by and large, people are where they've quite consciously decided to be. That's life dude. Get used to it."

"But it's still open to her to change her destiny, is it not?"

"Well sure it is," replied Michael. "But she has to consciously make the decision to change as well, you know. And the change doesn't come overnight. Getting into predicaments is much easier than getting out of them."

"You're right there, Michael."

"Making a conscious decision to rob a bank," explained Michael, "is exactly the same as the conscious decision to chain yourself to debt for ten years. Well, in some respects anyway. Of course, one way involves breaking the law and the other doesn't. But both are decisions made consciously. Both, in this example, might have adverse effects. And, still yet, both might have serious repercussions well into the future. Both have real effects on stifling personal goals—should any goals be present. Maybe, though, those two paths I spoke of are those peoples' real course in life. Maybe that's what they decided their one shot at life will be. Not everyone has goals you know. Some people just exist and it bothers them not one bit."

"Exist," repeated Doc. "That's the name I gave some of them Below—'Existers.' Unless they change, their entire life will be for nothing else and to do nothing else other than to exist. But Michael, just existing *does* bother some people—they want to follow their dreams, but they can't because of past decisions they've made. They're stuck, floundering and on cruise control. They're stuck in the Stuff Cycle."

"Ok, fine. So they're stuck. If you had one of these people Below as your assignment and you perceived that they wanted to change and follow their dreams, what would you do about it?"

Doc knew he was getting to the hard part. But, he had an answer. "Well, I would start with…"

Before Doc was able to finish his sentence Michael interrupted. "Patience. Is that what you were going to say?"

"Yes. How did you know?"

"I heard you thinking furiously as I walked up to meet you," Michael said smiling. "Metallica is loud, but not even their music can quiet an earnest mind hard at work."

"Yes, it would be through patience," confirmed Doc. "I know how patience would…"

"…help them," said Michael. "Yes, I also heard your argument as to how you think patience would help them. But refresh my memory, give me your salient points again."

"I would try to instill in them a sense of patience in their spending habits first. I would try to teach them the difference between 'doing without' and 'going without.' There's a difference you know."

"Is there now? And what would those differences be?"

"Of course there's a difference," Doc started his explanation. "Someone can 'do without' without having to 'go without.'"

"That's a lot of 'withouts,'" laughed Michael.

Doc continued without missing a beat. "'Doing without' means that you have all you really need—oh sure, you can buy extras and luxuries now and then when you can afford them—but you really can 'do without' that new piece of stuff if you really had to. 'Going without'—or 'went without' if you're referring to a different tense—really refers to something more substantial like, say, food or clothing. Like when I was Below, my mom always, always made sure we never 'went without' but we 'did without' all the time. I guess that's because she knew that some stuff really wasn't that important and we could 'do without' it. It's a shame really that more people Below don't know the difference between 'doing without' and 'going without.'"

Michael was impressed. Doc did not disappoint in his first Observational Period.

Doc, on a roll, continued. "If I had as my assignment Below one of these people who was in debt to such a degree that it was preventing them from at least trying to follow what they thought would be their destination in life, then somehow I would try to teach them patience and guide them in exercising restraint."

"Now, how exactly do you propose to do that?" Michael asked trying to keep Doc going on his roll.

"I would do it through communication. Get them to listen to me…" said Doc confidently and very matter-of-factly, not wanting to give the Archangel a hint that he didn't quite yet know how to communicate with them, "…through signs," Doc said as an afterthought. Actually, using signs had not popped into his head until just that moment. "Yes, I would do it through signs."

"Signs, eh? What signs? How would these *signs* you speak of get through to the One Below?" asked Michael.

There was silence for a moment.

"I haven't got that far yet. But I know if patience and restraint could be taught and used for this problem by the people who wanted to change their life course, then I know, *I just know* that they would also see the benefits in using patience in other aspects of their lives."

"Liiiike?"

"Well, I don't know…perhaps if people used patience when it came to their finances, then maybe they would think twice about other things too…I don't know…like marriage…or choosing a job…or spouting off at a public meeting before they gave their brain time to evaluate what their mouth was going to say… I don't know, Michael, I don't have answers for everything you know," Doc said as he was becoming a little frustrated and just a touch upset with Michael for all his pushing. He was just about ready to let loose a few choice words on the Archangel to let him know that he didn't have the answers to all life's problems and that he really didn't appreciate all his pushing.

Seeing Doc becoming a little uncomfortable, Michael chipped in with a few of his own words on patience. "Delay is the best remedy for anger you know, Doc."

Doc looked at Michael and said nothing for a few seconds. Patience. Delay. Doc laughed. Those few seconds were enough to quell Doc's rising emotions. He's bested me, thought Doc. "Yeah, delay…that works also," said Doc slightly embarrassed.

They each looked at the other and chuckled a little.

Doc was hoping that Michael wouldn't bring up the question of *how* he intended to employ those signs or *what* signs he intended on using to help those Below who needed some guidance in the craft of patience.

Looking into Doc's overwhelmed eyes, Michael could tell he

wasn't quite ready for the *how* or the *what* part just yet. No matter, Michael thought to himself as he smiled at his young student, he's made great progress so far. I don't think any Senior got 'patience' after only one Observational Period.

"Usually, it takes at least two, sometimes even three, and even at that rate," Michael said as he continued his thoughts out loud while looking off into the distance, "three is seen as being a job well done."

"Takes two what? What job well done?"

"Huh?" replied Michael looking back at Doc. "Oh, nothing, nothing, just blabbering on to myself. So what's next on your agenda for Observational Period number two?"

"I'm not exactly sure," replied Doc. "I made a point of observing as many people Below as I could during my first Period because being a Basic and Junior you really only get a chance to watch one person at any given time. So, I don't know, maybe my focus for my next Period will be back to watching individuals again. Although this time being alive to more of what's really going on in their lives. I really don't know yet. I'll figure it out. Whatever it is, I hope I don't see so much mindless consumption like I did during my first Period. That is a complete and utter shame. Not to mention a complete and utter waste of time."

Doc was just about to start in on what he meant by mindless consumption, how many people bought into mindless activity and that it was whiling away their precious time Below. And, the fact that many people seemed not to care.

"Tell me about it," Michael said without prompting. "Isn't it awful? The waste. Just think about what could be accomplished in the amount of time that people are glued to *Temptation City* or logged onto myspacebook.com...or whatever it is they're watching. Who knows...well, He knows...oh, and I know...but other than the two of us, who knows how many potential world leaders, rock stars, bowlers, hobby carpenters or really good fathers and mothers are wasting their life watching stuff?"

Doc thought for a moment.

"Well, Michael, did you ever think that all those people are doing exactly what they want to do? Maybe there are no future rock stars or pilots that are addicted to reality shows because their destiny in life isn't to be a leader or a doer...it's to live out their life just existing, eh? Did you ever think of that?"

The Archangel laughed in spite of himself. "Touché, my boy." Doc chuckled along with him, but the question that he wanted an answer most for was still unanswered.

Doc wanted to ask how he did in his first Observational Period. Did I pass? thought Doc. Why won't he tell me? Oh well, I suppose no news is good news and I'm sure he'll tell me when he's good and ready to tell me.

He was starting to get to know the Archangel and his odd behaviour a little better now. Doc genuinely liked Michael. Not just because he was the highest Angel and Archangel and God's Counsel, but because he really enjoyed learning from Michael. He made it fun. Learning, thought Doc, is so much better...and easier...when it's fun. Remembering his time Below, he was very thankful that he had been taught by so many great teachers and professors who were really more than great teachers—they were great people. Too bad more teachers didn't see it that way.

And, he was truly thankful that he just happened to stumble across Michael that day when the Archangel was talking with Edmund.

Why was it that I met him *that* day? The Academy could have informed me that Michael would be conducting my Interviews and I was to report to him after ten days. That could have happened. Huh, I guess Michael was right, everything does happen for a reason.

"Hey Michael," Doc said as he was finishing his thought that everything happens for a reason and interrupting Michael whistling some Guns N' Roses song, "remember you said everything happens for a reason?"

"Yes, I remember, back on page...oh, what was it? Paaage...ah, I can't remember. No matter, yes, I remember," Michael said in between bars in his song.

"Page? What page? We were talking, not reading a book," said Doc, as he was trying to figure out what song Michael was whistling.

"Yes, page. I know we were having a conversation at the time, but conversations are a lot like books. Sometimes you have conversations for fun. Sometimes you have conversations in the hopes of learning something. Some books you read for fun or entertainment as it were and other books you read to learn something. So, if our conversation had been a book, it would have been on page…32 or whatever. Get my drift?"

"Suuure," Doc said if for no other reason than to agree with the Archangel. "Anyway, you do remember saying that everything happens for a reason, right?"

"Right."

"Everything?"

"Yup, pretty much," replied Michael. "Why?"

"Oh, I don't know, it's something that I always believed myself but wasn't really sure why. Other than…it happened for a reason… because whatever it was that happened, happened because it was supposed to."

"Sounds like a bad case of circular reasoning to me, Doc," Michael said with a raised eyebrow. "Things always happen for a reason. Why? Because they're supposed to. Is that what you think?"

"Kind of," replied Doc, knowing that things usually did happen for a reason, but wasn't sure why. "But why do some things happen and other things not?" That was a pretty broad question and Doc knew it, but he thought that if Michael could at least shed some light on the matter then maybe he could figure it out from there.

"Well, yes, you will come to learn that everything does happen for a reason. Make no mistake about that. Like you, many down Below believe this also. They're right. Things do happen for a reason."

"Yes, but why?" asked Doc, "I'm after the 'why' of it all."

"Sometimes there is no 'why?' There just is," said Michael as plainly as he could. "Sometimes the reason is apparent within seconds of it happening…sometimes it's not apparent for many years. Sometimes the reason is deep, only to be uncovered and realized upon the occurrence of other happenings. Sometimes the reason is trivial…even logical…maybe very simple. Which, for the purposes of our deeper discussion, really amounts to no reason at all. It all depends on what meaning you give the word 'reason.' Everything is relative lad."

This got Doc thinking.

Everything happens for a reason, but sometimes it amounts to no reason at all, repeated Doc in his mind. "How's that?" asked Doc.

"Which one do you want to talk about first—the fact that everything happens for a reason, or the fact that the reason why some things happen amounts to no reason at all…and thereby void of any really deeper meaning?" asked Michael.

"The one where you say that things happen for a reason, which amounts to no reason at all…let's start with that one," replied Doc anxiously.

"Very well…did you eat today?" asked Michael breaking from his whistling.

Doc laughed. "Is this another test?"

"Doc, my boy, humour me. You asked the question. After a moment or three you might see where I'm going."

"Ok…yes, I did eat today."

"Why?"

"Because I was hungry."

"When you walked here today, did you come by way of the path the entire way or did you cut across the lawn in front of the Cathedral?" Michael asked with a raised eyebrow.

Oops, I didn't think anybody was watching. "Uh…walked across the lawn. But it wasn't for very long. No, really. Just to cut off 100 feet or so. I didn't want to be late. I wasn't sure if you were waiting or how patient you'd be for my arrival." Doc hoped he wasn't going to get in trouble.

"And there are your answers," said Michael, almost oblivious to the fact that no one was supposed to be walking across the lawn at the Cathedral. At least, the part where the signs said "Keep Off Grass" which is exactly the spot where Doc had walked.

"What answers?" Doc was now trying to remember what the question was.

"The reason why some things happen sometimes amounts to no reason at all and thereby is void of any deeper meaning...that answer. You ate, because you were hungry. You walked across the lawn instead of taking the path because you didn't want to be late. Both of those things happened for a reason, yet, really, they happened for no deeper reason other than you were just responding to how you were feeling."

"Gotcha," replied Doc. "Ok, what about why things happen for a real reason, a reason that does have deeper meaning?"

"That depends."

"On what?" asked Doc.

"It depends on a lot of things. Like who it's happening to Below. Like who that person's Guardian Angel is. It depends where they're taking their life. It depends on what's going on in their life at that time. It depends on a whole host of things. And what comes of the event or the happening, the outcome or aftermath as it were, depends on many things as well."

"How so?" asked Doc hanging on to each and every word the Archangel was saying. These are the things, thought Doc, I really want to learn.

"Well, sometimes the reason is complex, very complex, and un-knowable...the reason that is, to anyone Below...except to those who are the most adept at interpreting such things. Things that happen which have underlying deeper meanings—whether the thing happening is a good thing or bad thing—sometimes are only capable of being seen for what they really are by the very perceptive. I don't know...call them signs if you want. If something happens Below—something that has a deeper meaning—sometimes it's viewed as a sign by the person it happened to in order to get them to act upon it. Complex stuff isn't it?"

"Uh huh," said Doc, trying to make sense of it all.

"And, to add to the confusion, sometimes the littlest thing can have the deepest meaning. Anyone can interpret a huge, meaningless event—almost anyone that is—but sometimes seemingly little inconsequential events happen for a huge reason. The key is to know how to interpret them."

He was slowly getting it. I need to think more about that one, Doc thought. A review of some of my Senior Theory notes might come in handy tonight.

But he wasn't so concerned about little events turning into big events. He would have time to figure that one out. The reason why he asked the question about why things happened and why it was that everything happened for a reason was predicated on death.

Death is such a hard subject to grasp, thought Doc. Why do some people die early, untimely deaths and others don't? Why do some outlive others when there is no logical explanation for it? This confounded Doc up Here and during his time Below.

I might as well, he thought, gathering the nerve to ask Michael's opinion on such a mysterious subject—get right to the point.

"What about untimely deaths?" asked Doc. "Why do they happen?"

"Untimely deaths...what, you don't want to talk anymore about why it was you ate this morning?" said Michael somewhat surprised at Doc's leap from food to death.

"I already know why I ate this morning, but I don't know why some people die when they do, especially when it just doesn't seem right."

"Alright...well, for starters, and looking at the big picture, untimely deaths happen for exactly the same reason why all deaths happen. And that is because that is *exactly* what was supposed to happen. That's the reason...the over-arching reason. In the abstract, if you get my meaning," Michael said, knowing that the big picture really wasn't the context to which Doc was referring.

"The big picture?"

"Yes, the big picture," replied Michael. "All deaths happen exactly when they're supposed to because, quite simply, that's the way it is. Suffice it to say that all deaths happen exactly when they're supposed to. Period. Just like everybody Below is at a certain point in their life because that's exactly where they're supposed to be at that given time. However, there is one major difference. The people Below can change, if they want, where they are going in the future, but only He knows when that person is going to die. Obviously, sometimes people lead themselves down the road to death willingly, but only He knows when their time has come. So, yes, in a sense, untimely deaths happen right when they're supposed to just like natural deaths…for lack of a better term."

"Ok, so untimely deaths happen right when they're supposed to just like regular deaths, right? But that tells me nothing of the 'why' though. *Why* do untimely deaths happen?"

"The reasons could be numerous," Michael replied. "Do you want me to give you every single life scenario that's possible of being played out Below and it's accompanying infinite number of reasons for why it happened?"

"No, just one will do," said Doc with a smile.

"Just one," asked Michael, "not two?"

"One will do," said Doc politely.

"Very well. For instance, one reason…and I repeat, one reason… for an untimely death was that it was God's will."

"I think you already mentioned that, Michael. But give me one *reason* for God's will in a case like that."

The reason for God's will, thought Michael flabbergasted. "The reason for God's will?" repeated Michael out loud. "I'm Michael, the Archangel, God's Counsel, one who is *like* God…not God Himself. How should I know? Ask God. I'm only First Among Equals…well, we already went over that little piece of legal fiction, but I'm only an Angel, Doc, not the Almighty."

"Yeah, but you know what I mean. You know why sometimes untimely deaths happen, and I'm not talking about the big picture. I'm talking about the little picture. The picture that matters to family members Below when a loved one dies in the prime of their life and they are left searching for answers about why it happened," said Doc with a little more assertiveness. "What are some of the potential reasons why untimely deaths happen? I know you know, Michael."

"Yes, I know," Michael replied quietly. His whistling had stopped. He paused. "Just one?"

"Yeah, I promise, just one."

"On occasion, God will permit, or at least not prevent, a seemingly untimely death Below because he has deemed that person will serve a better purpose up Here. Oh, and just so you know, sometimes He—or *we*—will step in and prevent a death...but you already knew that, Mr. Traffic Diversion King. And by the way, what seems as 'untimely' Below, is very timely in His eyes—just so you're clear on that."

"What do you mean, 'serve a better purpose'?"

"Well, it might be so that God can employ that person as a Guardian Angel quicker than usual. The person might be taken away from Below early—when viewed by others from Below—because God has decided that this person would be perfectly suited to take on the role of Guardian. It's hard, I know, for people Below to come to terms with that, but it's a fact."

Doc was listening intently. Doc's chickadee friend that had been singing and playing tag with a dragonfly all morning perched itself on the back of the bench right next to Doc's shoulder. The dragonfly landed on Michael's knee; Edmund was in his hand. All four waited silently for the Archangel to start up again.

"Perhaps, and it's only a perhaps, as in it's the reason sometimes but not all the time...so perhaps, God sees that the future for that person Below might be dominated by despair and for one reason or another the person will be unable to escape it. Then, knowing that the person will be unable to overcome what lies ahead—and don't forget, at this time what the future brings is unbeknownst to the person or his family—sometimes God will bring that person up Here to avoid the future. Seemingly bad things happen to good people. In this case, the life Below is taken long before the despair happens in order to completely pre-empt the earthly suffering. When this occurs, others Below are grief-stricken and second-guess God's benevolence because they see no reason for the apparent sense-less death. But God knows otherwise. Or, at other times, the suffer-ing and despair will have already started and God calls them Home in the middle of it because He knows that for whatever reason, the person won't be able to find their way out of it."

"Either way," Michael continued, "God has stepped in and spared the person Below unimaginable suffering to bring the person into His employ. Untimely Below, but very, very timely for God. Indeed, it's an example of His own perfect execution of His perfect will. So there...there is one reason for deaths that seem untimely Below. There are others and I have no doubt that you will learn them in time. Remember Doc, the more you learn, the better you'll be at serving your assignment Below. The more knowledge you have about things such as this the better you'll be at sending signs and communicating with your assignment in order to help them. We'll have to work on signs and communication at some point."

Death, Doc thought, is such a hard thing to understand. Michael's reason made him feel a little better. "Thanks Michael, that helps me out a bit. What about the reason why someone lives to be ninety-five or a hundred?"

Michael moved closer to Doc and looked in his ears. He looked bewilderedly at Edmund and the chickadee as if to ask them if he heard Doc's question correctly. Then he stuck a finger in his own ears. Michael was almost positive that they agreed on him giving just *one* example of why things happen.

"I'm sorry, perhaps my ears aren't working, or maybe it's yours that aren't working, but I thought we agreed on 'just one' reason why things happened?"

"No," Doc replied with a smile, "on page...oh whatever page it was, I can't remember now...it doesn't matter...anyway, back on page whatever...that's if our conversation was a book, a learning book, you know that conversations in some instances parallel books don't you, Michael? Yes, well, anyway, I said give me just one reason why 'untimely deaths' happen...not just one reason why *anything* happens."

Michael started to laugh, but he wasn't going to give up the fight yet. "No, *Doc*, I said I would give you just one reason why every-thing happened for a reason. I know what I said and don't you try and twist my words...besides, I know th..."

"I know that delay is the best remedy for anger," Doc said grin-ning from ear to ear just as Michael was getting a little hot under the collar.

Speechless, Michael quickly looked at Doc then turned away. Both started chuckling. Michael became, in a fun sort of way, a little annoyed. And with his hair all over the place from playing along to Metallica, he looked rather funny.

"Fine, fine," Michael said giving up, "what was your *second* ques-tion again?"

"Why some people live to be a hundred?"

"Because, they're healthy...so there," replied Michael. "Or it's be-cause they've discovered the fountain of youth. There, there's two answers for your *second* question. I've got to be going. Edmund and I have someplace to go."

"Oh no you don't, Edmund's doing just fine where he is. Look, he's fine right where he is. It doesn't look to me that he's in a rush to get anywhere. For once, he's not hurrying or jumping about. In fact, he looks like he's rather enjoying this."

When Doc and Michael started into their playful banter, Edmund started grinning and by now was almost doubled over with laughter. "Look at him, he's in no rush to get going anywhere."

"How would Edmund know where we're supposed to be...he's only a chipmunk."

Michael looked down at Edmund. There was Edmund on his back, laughing away, kicking his legs in the air. "Edmund," Michael said somewhat sternly, "stop your laughing, immediately...or there'll be no more cake for you." The more Michael raised his voice, the more Edmund laughed. And laughed even more because Michael's rock star hair was everywhere. Meanwhile, the chickadee and the dragonfly flew off to resume their game of tag. They had had enough of the nonsense.

"Hmmph…chipmunks," Michael said in a huff, looking at Edmund. Then he looked at Doc. "Hmmph, Seniors…oh, very well, you win. Why do some people live to be a hundred as opposed to suffering an early death—is that your question?"

"The one and the same." Learning can be so much fun, thought Doc.

"Alright…well, as you know, some people live to be very old. Yes, God sees to that sometimes. Take for instance, say…a grandmother, who lives to be ninety-five or so."

"Why a grandmother?" asked Doc.

"Because it's my hypothetical scenario and I get to pick the facts and the characters, that's why."

"Ok…a grandmother."

"As I was saying, sometimes a grandmother will live until the age of ninety-five…or whatever… Oh, by the way, grandmothers are the most important people Below. More important than world leaders. More important than musicians…more important than doctors. Sorry, no offence, Doc," Michael said apologetically.

"None taken."

"Yes, grandmothers are more important than any other identifi-able group whether you're talking about types of professions, types of people or whatever," Michael explained.

Doc remembered that his grandmother was a very important part of his life Below, but other than the personal bond between them, he wasn't sure why Michael was saying that they were the most impor-tant group of people Below. "Why grandmothers?" Doc asked.

"Love," said Michael. "God's love for them and their love for others."

"Love?"

"Love…" repeated the Archangel with affectionate authority.

"...because they give their love unconditionally to their grandchildren—no matter what. And, they bring complete joy to all those around them."

"Children," continued Michael, "can give their parents fits and starts for five out of five days, yet when they go to Grandma's house she welcomes them with hugs that have no equal, followed quickly with treats and perhaps a dollar or two. All for no other reason than because they are her grandchildren and she loves them unconditionally. Really loves them. Of course, parents do too. But it's different. It's grandmotherly love. It's a different kind of love. It just is."

Doc listened intently. Edmund was back to listening also.

"Actually, it's not well known," Michael kept on, "but grandmotherly love is a scientific fact. God made sure of that. Just the way He made the sun rise in the east. As sure as the solar system and how it operates is part of His way, so is grandmotherly love a part in His earthly order. He made it so. The capacity of grandmotherly love knows no bounds. He saw to it. And the real beauty of grandmothers, besides the obvious, is their ability to love while asking for nothing in return. Nothing. Oh sure, they love getting a thank you card recognizing a birthday present she gave them or they love getting masterful pieces of Grade One art for their fridge, but they truly ask for nothing in return. That's because they get just as much joy out of giving their love as their grandchildren do in receiving it. Ever heard the phrase 'It's better to give than to receive'?"

"Sure," said Doc.

"Well, it has its roots in a grandmother's love for her grandchildren. Understand a grandmother's love—not only to her grandchildren, but to everybody—and you will have come a great deal closer to understanding the concept of love in the abstract. I can't explain it any better than that. That's just the way it is. Besides, they're sweet too. And it's an utter shame that the younger don't pay more attention to grandmothers—and the elderly in general."

"Hmmm...I see," said Doc pondering the concept of grandmotherly love.

"Now, where was I? Oh yes, why God sometimes lets someone live until they're ninety-five as opposed to permitting a seemingly untimely death."

"Never mind...I got it. You have a knack for teaching in parables. Who taught you how to do that anyway?"

Michael said nothing; he just smiled. He liked it when Doc got it. He was on his way to becoming a great Senior. "Doc, my friend, now I *really* have to go. No, really"

"Sure, Michael, sorry for keeping you so long—I didn't mean to." Doc stood up, getting ready to leave.

"No trouble at all, my boy...all in the name of education right? So, we're all set for our next meeting?" Michael asked.

"Yeah, I guess so," said Doc, "...same time, same place?"

"Sure, if you like. Ten days hence?"

"Eleven, if you don't mind...I was going to go over some Senior Theory notes tomorrow and then start my Observational Period the day after next...if that's ok with you?"

"Not a problem. The extra day will give me some more time to prepare my opening speech for the 'N' Debate. I'm not a questioner this time around—just the keynote speaker. It should be a good lineup though—Nelson vs. Napoleon...round two, as it were. Ok, dude...see you then."

"See you later, Michael," Doc said as he waved goodbye.

Each walked his own way and Edmund fell in behind the Archangel. Doc turned back for another quick goodbye wave just in time to see Edmund run up the back of Michael's right leg, onto his hip, up his arm and then into his hand. As the two of them walked away—one in hand—Doc heard the Archangel start whistling again. Edmund was swaying from side to side with the music. Finally Doc recalled the name of the song that Michael had been whistling: "Patience" by Guns N' Roses.

Hmmm, thought Doc, patience indeed.

As Doc turned around again and headed home, he was replaying the conversation he had with Michael: patience, signs, communication, death, grandmotherly love. I've learned a lot today, Doc said to himself, but I still feel like there's so much more to learn. Doc quickly turned around to see if the Archangel heard his circular thoughts. Michael was long out of sight.

Eager to learn more, Doc headed for home. He still hadn't made up his mind where or to what end he would focus next, but perhaps, he thought, his notes would give him some ideas.

That night Doc crawled into bed savouring the fresh smell of just-washed sheets. Doc's cleaning lady was great.

II

STUDY BREAKS

The next morning, Doc got out of bed and put on some old clothes
for hanging around the house. His comfortable clothes of choice for
reading or weeding his garden were usually ripped jeans, a t-shirt
and a baseball cap—always on backwards. After dressing he walked
from his bedroom, into the hall, through his living room, which was
lined with bookshelves and more bookshelves, and into the kitchen.
After eating a quick bowl of fresh fruit his cleaning lady had pre-
pared the night before, he made his morning cup of coffee. Sitting
himself down in his favourite reclining chair—his only chair—he
grabbed his Senior Theory notes and made himself comfortable.

Doc went over various subjects and concepts: the art of unspoken
communication, classification of people Below, signs, TANAHI and

others. He also rehashed what he saw during his first Observational Period and his understanding of patience. As well, Doc thought about the things he and the Archangel had spoken about: death and grandmothers.

Death. Doc thought a lot about death. Untimely ones; natural ones. Seemingly senseless deaths and deaths—if such a thing was possible—that made sense. It's true, he thought, everyone dies. God sees to that. But not everyone really *lives*—people themselves have to see to that. Living a truly meaningful life, and not just existing, was entirely in the hands of the Ones Below. The more he thought about death and living, and existing, the more he wanted to learn what his role in all of this would be. A role that a Basic and a Junior never really had to fill.

He spent the entire day going over his notes and texts—only breaking for lunch and the odd break where he invariably found himself outside weeding his garden, talking and listening.

The weeding, no matter how often he did it, usually was not quite enough to make his gardens perfect. However, Doc wasn't after the perfect garden. He was content with making his hostas, Sweet Williams and daisies look tended and cared for. Pulling every weed every day meant more trips to the 'Weed Garden'—the home where all weeds went after being pulled. Everything had a place Above.

The talking he engaged in was with the birds that seemed to frequent his place more than the places of other Angels that he knew. Maybe they like to hang out here because I talk to them. They need conversation too…and I guess feeding them doesn't hurt either, figured Doc.

And, he listened. To his soul.

Those three things were what Doc did with most of his spare time and they provided a comforting respite from studying. He learned from all three.

When he finally decided it was time to get some sleep he still hadn't figured out what he would concentrate on observing during his next Period. It'll come to me tomorrow, he thought, it always does. Just like when I was Below. He started to remember that when things weren't quite right—then things weren't done yet. The end hadn't yet arrived. If you give yourself time to consciously and conscientiously—there was a difference, he reminded himself—to work things out, then they almost always would. Taking comfort in that, Doc fell asleep.

12

Blame it on God

Doc awoke eager to start his Second Observational Period. "But not before I've had a nice steaming-hot cup of coffee and a quick read. I think I'll go out for coffee today," he said aloud to himself, still laying in bed and savouring his nice-smelling sheets.

He still didn't have a game plan for his second Observational Period. "Perhaps when I'm observing I'll find out what to concentrate on," Doc said as he continued his solo conversation. "After all, you don't always know where you're going or what destination you're seeking when you start out," he said, trying to convince himself that by just pointing himself in the right direction and letting things unfold in front of him he would end up on the right course. Yes, that's it, he thought, as long as I kind of point myself in the right direction, then things will work out.

Doc got dressed and walked over to his favourite coffee shop; five paths, two forks and one turn from home.

He sat down with his back against the wall at his favourite table in the corner in his favourite chair on the front patio. This way, Doc always kept everything in front of him. As he sat down and breathed the fresh morning air, he thought, yes, a quick read and a cup of coffee will start me off just fine.

As the waiter walked by, Doc called out, "Hey Morty, how'ya doing? Maybe a medium—of the house special blend—and a *BEN* please. No time for a large today, I'm on my way…"

Morty cut his sentence short. "Yeah, I figured you wouldn't be staying long…in fact, I didn't think I'd see you at all over the next little bit. How are your Observational Periods going?"

"Oh, they're going ok…hey, how'd you know I was doing my Senior Observations?" Doc asked.

"It's my business to know the business of my customers…besides good news travels fast up Here, almost as fast as bad news travels Below," replied Morty with a wink.

As he was waiting for Morty to return, Doc noticed Edgar and Louise walking by. Edgar sold birdseed in Doc's neighbourhood and Louise looked after the "Weed Garden."

"Hey, Hawk…hey Weedy," Doc called over, using the nicknames he had given them. It was common knowledge Above that after meeting Doc, you would have a new nickname within a matter of days. These names, more often than not, stuck. Doc was the nick-name King.

"Hey, Doc," Hawk said as he returned the greeting. "You must be getting low on black sunflower…haven't seen you in awhile."

"I know, I know… Sorry, I'll be in shortly. I'm busy."

"We're busy, too," Weedy piped in. "Seems there's more weeds this year than others. Do you know how hard it is to separate the spotted knapweed from the milkweed? Each want to take over the whole garden. It's very busy being a weedener." Weedy laughed.

"We're all busy," Hawk said. "But just remember, feeding birds and weeding sometimes brings balance. We all need balance."

"I know, I know... I'll be in to see you soon." The three of them chatted for a couple of minutes until Hawk and Weedy had to get going. Doc wondered if Hawk was courting Weedy.

In a few minutes, Morty returned with Doc's order, "One medium house special and today's copy of *BEN*. I had a quick look at it before work...nothing much new Below."

Doc took a sip of his coffee and started to read the front page of *BEN: The Below Earthly News. The Below Earthly News* was one of the largest circulation papers Above that covered news Below. The paper enjoyed a large readership of Guardian Angels. It was important for Guardian Angels to be aware of various developments Below. *BEN* gave a good quick overview of some newsworthy events Below, presenting—as papers go, and to such an extent as was possible—a fairly unbiased view.

Doc flipped from page to page. Huh, he thought, Morty was right, not much new today. Doc kept flipping but he saw most of the same. There were stories of greed evidenced in the numerous corporate scandals. More stories on greed evidenced in the scandals done at the hands of politicians. Western countries—including Canada, Doc noted—seemed to have their fair share of political scandals. And, there were yet more stories on greed, centred on the private sector. Just another typical newsday, thought Doc.

Halfway into the first section, a particular story caught Doc's attention: "Man's Misfortune Results in Government Inquiry." This ought to be interesting, thought Doc as he started to read the story:

A hard-working man laboured long hours in the summer putting away supplies for the upcoming winter. His neighbour laughed at him for working so hard and played the entire summer, nary putting any supplies away for the upcoming winter when food would be short and fuel for heat scarce.

During that winter the hard-working man was warm and

well fed. The neighbour was cold and hungry; he called his government representative and demanded to know why his neighbour should be allowed to be warm and never go hungry while the less fortunate like him were cold and starving.

The television media soon caught wind of the story and shot some live footage of the neighbour who was cold and hungry. The television station also showed footage of the hard-working man sitting in his chair by a nice roaring fire eating a hearty supper.

Much of the population became appalled that in a country of such seeming wealth a poor, unfortunate neighbour was allowed to suffer such hardships while others seemed to have plenty.

Various political parties, union members and lobbyists for different rights groups started to demonstrate in front of the hard-working man's house. The demonstrators claimed that the hard-working man got rich off the misfortune of his neighbour. They called for an immediate tax hike.

In response, the government drafted new retroactive taxation policies. The new taxation policies took much of the hard-working man's savings that he had worked so hard to build up. The hard-working man was also fined for not hiring his neighbour as a worker. Nothing was mentioned about the fact that the hard-working man offered his neighbour a job, but he refused. Because the hard-working man did not have enough money to pay both the fine and the new taxes, his home was confiscated by the government. Of course, the neighbour didn't have to pay any of the new taxes because he had no job. Yet, there were jobs to be had.

The hard-working man moved to a different country and through hard work started another successful business.

The neighbour, now on government assistance provided for by the new taxes levied on the hard workers, is now fat and warm. The neighbour now lives in the hard-working man's confiscated house because it is now owned by the government and used for government housing. However, the neighbour doesn't keep the house in good repair and it starts to fall apart.

The country's news media now blames the house's disrepair on inadequate government funding. The government, not knowing what to do, called a commission of inquiry at a cost of millions of dollars paid for by the hard-working citizens. The neighbour was supposed to give evidence at the commission's hearing but he died of a drug overdose before he could give his testimony. It is rumoured that his testimony would be that he was very upset that the government allowed him to live in such substandard housing.

The media blamed the neighbour's misfortune on the failure of the government to fix the root causes of despair and poverty arising from social inequity.

Now empty, the house is abandoned and eventually had to be torn down. Not wanting to pay the property taxes anymore on the house, the government sold it for one dollar to bunch of criminals, who immediately started distributing marijuana to local kids because marijuana was now decriminalized in that country.

Doc rolled his eyes and grunted. Hmmph, Doc groaned, I guess some things never change. Just like the way when I lived Below... always some people blaming their misfortune on somebody else. Blamers...huh...there's another type of people.

Doc flipped through the rest of the paper, finished his coffee and went on his way, ready to start his second Observational Period. After reading the paper, Doc thought that he would check in on other facets of public life Below. Maybe, I can learn more about how people live and think if I observe what their governments are doing. Governments, after all, should be a good role model for the private sector. Doc started out his second Observational Period looking in on government.

He went from one government department to the next: the Finance Department, the Defence Department, the Health Department, the Justice Department and so on.

To his surprise, although he wasn't quite as surprised as he first thought, Doc found that people in government were becoming expert blamers and over-spenders. Elected government representatives were the best at blaming others for their misdeeds. And, whenever slack needed to be taken up, hand-picked top bureaucratic employees filled in wonderfully.

No one was taking responsibility for anything. If there was over-spending, it was due to an accounting or clerical error—not the fact that no one in the department had a handle on the control of their budget. If government contracts were given out illegally, everybody claimed ignorance or that they were just taking orders from someone else. That someone else said that they knew nothing about it and they were just taking orders from someone else. And so the merry-go-round continued. Nobody ever stood up and admitted their mistakes.

It seems to me there's a culture of blaming around government today…nobody ever has to account for anything. No wonder the citizenry blames their misfortune on everybody else. They're only doing what their government officials are doing, thought Doc.

Whether it was overspending or illegal transactions, everybody, especially elected representatives, were blaming others.

The next day, Doc peered in to have a look at private life again to see if the culture of blame in the private lives of people Below was as rife there as it was in government. Doc found that it was.

This person blamed his inability to work a regular job because of something his Grade 5 teacher said in class one day that haunted him for years. That person blamed his failed marriage on the fact that his wife spent all their savings on bingo and video lottery games and no one stepped in to stop it. Another person blamed her poor health on a hamburger company for not warning her that eating hamburgers five times a week and sitting on the couch would make her fat; she then blamed the government for not banning hamburgers. A kid blamed his parents for not letting him go out to a school dance just because he bullied a classmate at school who had a nice ball cap that he wanted. A human rights group blamed the school for fostering inequality by allowing the "fortunate and rich" kid to wear his nice ball cap to school—incidentally, a cap that he bought with his *own* money from delivering newspapers.

My goodness, thought Doc, people Below have gotten to the point where they want to be protected from everything...they want to be protected from themselves. What on earth is going on? These people Below are blaming everything and anything on others.

The next night, Doc observed the home life of one of the government's elected representatives. The elected representative's son handed his father a letter from the school principal. The letter stated that the son had stolen another child's chocolate bar and as a consequence he would have detention for one hour every day next week after school.

"But Dad," the son said, "it wasn't me. It was...it was...the new kid."

"Son," the father said, knowing that his son *did* take the chocolate bar, "you made a mistake. Everybody makes mistakes. Be a big person and admit to that mistake, say you're sorry and don't do it again."

"Ok, Dad, I'm sorry, it won't happen again. Promise."

"There, that's better. Now, do your detention next week and let this be a lesson to you."

Doc shook his head. Geesh, these people Below are telling their kids to do the right thing then when it comes to their time, they revert back to their expert blaming ways. It must be an age thing, the older you get the less responsibility for your actions you have to take.

Having seen enough blame to last a lifetime, Doc headed for home and bed. He didn't even open his Senior Theory notes for a quick review.

Oh well, if I don't pass my Interviews I'll just blame it on God. Hmmm, blame it on God...He might as well be blamed for something because everyone else is being blamed.

Blame it on God.

13

time is Life

Doc was up early the next day to continue his observing. He saw a great deal this day: more Blamers and more Existers. He wondered how many of the people in these groups believed in God and therefore had Guardian Angels watching over them.

He also remembered something that Michael had said during one of their previous conversations. '*Maybe*,' Doc remembered the Archangel's words, '*her true calling was to be in debt and have lots of stuff and never have to do without. Maybe that's her destiny. Maybe it's her husband's destiny too.*'

Doc thought about that. Maybe it was also somebody's lot in life to blame everybody for everything that happened. That way they could just exist and blame and not have to worry about doing anything positive themselves. Kind of an easy way out, thought Doc.

But he still wasn't convinced that blaming everybody for your woes was the right path to follow.

He remembered another thing Michael had said very early on in their first conversation. Michael had said, '*God is always willing to let people—of all various states of existence—prove their worth, Below and up Here. He will always give you ample opportunity. It's up to you to seize it—wherever you are.*'

Doc was trying to make sense of it all.

If these people are so unhappy with their lot in life, why don't they change it? Why do they blame? Why do they just barely exist? Why do they waste so much time being beholden to *stuff*? The Seekers I saw, or at least the people who I think are Seekers, don't blame. They *do*. And even the people that are content and truly happy don't blame either. I'd like to meet a Seeker.

Doc figured it was a conscious decision—for whatever reason— that those people Below were making as to how to live their lives. But they didn't get to such a state in one day. They didn't find themselves blaming everybody overnight. They didn't find themselves in debt overnight. And, Doc thought, the people who were happy, content or even seeking, didn't get there overnight either. No, those people worked hard over many years to realize the fruit of their hard work. Pearl Jam, The Who and Rush, he thought, didn't become planetary rock stars in a week. Search and rescue pilots didn't learn to fly helicopters over a weekend. It took them years of hard work. Doc figured that the Blamers and Existers worked at doing their chosen craft over a period of time too.

Doc was slowly piecing it all together.

Everybody, I think, is the master of their own destiny. That was God's plan. Or at least part of it. God let everyone Below follow the life and path that they wanted to follow. If you wanted to be a Blamer, people Below were free to follow that path. Same thing for Existers. If they wanted to live their life knowing nothing more than debt and having "stuff," then they were at liberty to do that too. Those who were content or Seekers were free to be happy and follow their goals. Everyone, with a few exceptions, are totally in command of their lives and they could live it anyway they saw fit.

Perhaps Michael was right, Doc thought, maybe it was the destiny of some Below to just exist, surrounded by stuff, while they blamed others for not being able to get ahead…or to be happy.

On his last night of observing Doc made sure he visited some happy people. He was pleased to find many who were content with their lives. Never doing anything unexpected, nor adventurous. Most of them really weren't living out their personal destiny or following their dreams. But they were definitely happy. Genuinely happy. For the most part they weren't in debt; they liked their jobs, had great friends, and were pretty much satisfied in their family life. They had hobbies and really seemed to enjoy life and the simple way in which they lived it.

Huh, not a bad way of living life…they seem truly content. Nothing wrong with being content. That's what I'll call them…the Content.

Doc finished out his second Observational Period, trying to reach a conclusion on his dilemma: why some people excelled and others floundered. As he was trying to figure that out, Doc thought that it had nothing to do with intelligence or education. You didn't have to be smart or have a university degree to be happy and content. You didn't have to have a particularly high IQ to be Content. Doc was slowly understanding what set the Content—and maybe Seekers—apart from the others…although he didn't quite know for sure. What he did know was that the Content were certainly not Existers or Blamers. Happiness seemed to play some kind of a role. Happiness wasn't predicated on how smart you are. Happiness doesn't just pick the smart people or rich people to attach itself to. Happiness and contentment do not discriminate, figured Doc.

"It's open to everybody," Doc said aloud to himself as he was walking home after his last night of observing, "to be happy, to be content, to seek out their goals. It's open to everyone to work hard towards a dream. Sure, it might take time, but all people have Below is time. That's what life is... *time*. Time to do what you want. Time is life."

He was preparing for what he would tell Michael. "It must come from within... Yes...that's it," said Doc as he neared home. "The drive to be content, happy and determined to seek out goals, comes from within. The soul and mind both must take an active part in directing and guiding the physical body towards happiness."

Happiness is hard work, thought Doc, that's why so many don't experience happiness...because it's hard work! It's far easier to blame others for your unhappiness than it is to work hard for your happiness. It's also far easier to exist and tolerate life than it is to work hard towards a fulfilling destination. People Below are taking the easy way out and thereby denying themselves true happiness. But because they've made the conscious decision to take the easy way out, then that might be their lot in life after all. Too bad, thought Doc, that many people Below were taking the easy way out... Hard work—it's not easy, he mused.

Pleased with the connections he was making and thinking about the things he would tell the Archangel the next day, Doc settled in to bed and sleep gradually overtook his thoughts.

14

MAD AS HECK

Doc was up early…he didn't want to cut across the lawn of the Cathedral again should Michael be early. He didn't think Michael would be early, but he wanted to get an early start just in case. With time to spare, Doc went to the coffee shop for a quick cup and a quick read. Morty wasn't busy and when he saw Doc approaching he had his coffee and paper waiting for him when he arrived.

"Thanks Morty…how you been?" Doc said, as he skimmed the pages of *BEN*.

"Fine, just fine…King Louie was just in. He wanted to wait for you, but he had to go. Something about checking in on his stable of royal steeds and did they need replacing and was this one too fat and should he put this one out to pasture because it didn't ride well anymore…and, well, you know…that's Louie. So, what's new?"

"Ah nothing," replied Doc, not really wanting to get into some of the troubling things he was observing. Doc quickly drank his coffee and read a few short news briefs. One article he read had some personal significance to him. It was an interview with the government representative that Doc had seen a few nights earlier teaching the value of admitting your mistakes to his son. The Above News Wire picked the story up from a paper Below and ran it in *BEN*. Doc read certain parts of the interview with keen interest:

"…but Sir…you were in charge of that department that lost millions of dollars of taxpayer's money. Not only that, now the money can't be accounted for. Hundreds-of-millions of dollars have been lost and are untraceable. Is that not your responsibility—to see to it that those things don't happen in your department?"

"Yes, I was in charge of that department. But I have no idea where the money went and besides I was taking direction from elected officials higher up and I was even taking direction from bureaucrats who were below me. I know nothing of what you speak of."

"Well," the reporter continued, "you were in charge of that program, and even staff members in your department said that they were taking orders from you. Where is the money? Where did it go? Where is the paperwork that was supposed to follow those transactions? Sources say that all the documents have been destroyed."

"Look it," started the elected politician as so many of his colleagues now started out their evasive answers, as if starting an obvious cover-up with a forceful word or two would somehow bring legitimacy to their answer. "Look it, I can tell you that I have no idea where the money went. I can even say I didn't run this program even though it was my department that was looking after disbursing the funds. I had direction from others."

"From who?" asked the reporter.

"I can't remember…all I know is that it is not my fault," finished off the elected politician. "Look it, I'm a politician and I'm interested in our county's values. I know nothing about how this program was run. And I'm mad as heck."

Doc had read enough. Indeed, you didn't know *anything* about it.

Doc figured that the missing millions of dollars not only got funneled back to his political party but also into the pockets of a few select people—probably even some elected officials. So much for taking responsibility.

After his coffee and morning read, Doc went to the meeting bench. No sign of Michael, but he did see Edmund come scurrying along towards him with a piece of paper in his mouth. The chipmunk jumped up on Doc's knee and motioned for him to read it.

Doc brother, sorry I can't make our meeting today. I have other matters to attend to. Go back for your third Observational Period and keep doing the same thing you've been doing. Open your eyes to what's really going on Below. Just like you did for your first two Periods. If my guess is right, I would say that you've just about come to the realization how all of this fits together…that you've come to the conclusion that everybody Below is free to do what they will. Good for you for seeing that there is an easy way out for those who want to take it and a hard way for those who want to be happy. You're doing great Doc. Keep up the good work.

Your pal,
Michael

As Edmund went on his way, Doc wondered what kept Michael. "Must be something important, eh Edmund?" Doc said to Edmund as he hurried down the path. "Oh well, I'm glad that he thinks I'm on the right track." Having even more time to spare now, Doc went back to the coffee shop for a longer cup of coffee. After he finished his coffee Doc headed home for lunch, some studying of Senior Theory notes and some weeding, talking and listening.

As Doc was proudly biting into one of his famous homemade roast beef, ham, turkey, tomato, pickle, cheese—minus the roast beef, ham, turkey, tomato, pickle—sandwiches, he opened up his Senior Theory notes. Doc fancied himself a good cook.

Patience, read Doc. "Well, I've got that one figured out, I think. Sometimes, if people Below would exercise some patience in their lives, then they wouldn't find themselves in some of the difficult situations they've gotten themselves into. Then, just like that woman Below, they might be able to follow their true calling. Their sadness didn't arrive in one fell swoop, they actually laid the groundwork for it months, sometimes years, in advance. Happiness really does take time to experience…just like unhappiness."

Doc was rehearsing his lines in case Michael ever asked him again. In extolling the virtues of patience, he had also figured out the cure for mid-life crises. "If people showed more patience and restraint in their younger years they wouldn't find themselves in mid-life crises so much."

"I think I have death figured out too," said Doc just before he went onto the next subject. "Everyone dies…God sees to that. But not everyone truly lives during the time they're given…people Below have to see to that." Still, Doc knew that he would probably never understand death *completely*. No one ever does, he said to himself silently. The best Doc could figure was that death could come unannounced at any time—like a thief in the night—so it's best to use your time Below wisely.

This one is still giving me some problems…the art of unspoken communication, Doc mumbled to himself as he read from his notes. I know that's where I come in and I know I have to somehow communicate with signs, but I'm not sure quite how yet.

Even when I do become adept at the art of unspoken communication and I learn how to guide and teach through signs…without going Below and showing myself…it's still up to my assignment Below to read those signs and act accordingly, wrote Doc in the margin of his notepaper. They must listen to me. Listen to my signs. My success, he continued writing, and the success of my assignment Below will be due in large part on how he or she is interpreting those signs and then acting in the proper way. Patience, thought Doc, I'll get it. Patience, wrote Doc on the top of his page.

"Yeah, like I know what TANAHI is. I have no idea what Temporary Apparent Non Association Human Intervention is. I guess I'll figure that one out as I go too."

"Classification of Ones Below," Doc read from a text as he switched from his notes. "I think I've got that one covered too. People Below can fit into certain categories," said Doc as he wrote down on a blank sheet of paper what those types were that he observed during his first two Periods: Blamers, Existers and the Content. "I know pretty much what they are, but I'm almost positive some people are Seekers. But I don't know what sets them apart. Heck, I haven't even observed one yet. If Michael hadn't mentioned I might get a Seeker as my next assignment I probably wouldn't even *know* there was such a thing."

Doc was feeling good about the progress he was making on the Senior learning curve. It was still early so Doc decided to go for a walk over to one of the Galleries. Each Gallery was but one spot where Guardian Angels gathered who were—at that moment—engaged in guarding, protecting, guiding and teaching. Maybe he could pick up some pointers on some of the things he was struggling with.

15

marco

Doc walked into the outside, open-air part of the Gallery. He saw many Guardian Angels at work. Some older, some younger ones. Some familiar faces, some faces he had never seen before. Sometimes Doc used a Gallery when he was actively guarding as a Basic or Junior, but at other times he just stayed home when he was so engaged. And still at other times, he would guard from wherever he happened to be at the moment when the guarding was needed: the coffee shop, the park or the symphony. Or, by his favourite spot, down by the water.

The Galleries had their advantages, insofar that Guardian Angels could swap stories and trade guarding techniques; but at times it became a noisy, boisterous hangout joint for Guardian Angels. Even still, Doc liked going there. The camaraderie was fun.

Doc parked himself in the open spot at the railing beside a distinguished looking Guardian Angel he hadn't met before. There were millions of Guardian Angels and Doc probably only knew half of them.

"Marco, Advanced," said the older Guardian Angel introducing himself to Doc.

"Doc, Senior Candidate," replied Doc as they shook hands.

"Oh, so you're the one I've heard so much about. Funny we haven't met yet, but after all there are millions of us," said Marco.

Why has everybody heard so much about me? Doc thought to himself. He still didn't get what all the fuss was about him. To him, he was just Doc. Nothing more, nothing less. Just Doc. Holy, I'm just me, you know.

"Yes, we are a lot aren't we…I guess that's a good thing," said Doc. "More belief in God Below I suppose."

"Yeah, but there's so many more of us in the Waiting Dock, ready for the call. Hopefully, as more people believe they'll be used too," Marco said a little louder in order to be heard over the laughs and shouts of the others.

"How did you know about me?"

"Ha…Michael was very proud that he aligned himself to do your Interviews and I guess he just had to get the word out. He told me the other day when I bumped into him at the cobbler shop. He's not the best at keeping secrets, you know. Besides there's not that many secrets up Here anyway."

"What are you doing Below right now?" Doc asked, eager to watch Marco and maybe pick up a pointer from an Advanced.

"Me? Right now, I'm just about to engage in TANAHI…but I have to wait for the opportune moment. A very difficult procedure. Not many can do it," said Marco proudly.

"Can I watch?"

"Sure…I think I'll be able to go down in about five minutes. Timing is everything."

"Go down...you mean Below? I thought that wasn't allowed," asked Doc.

"Oh...I see that you and Michael haven't gotten that far yet in your Interviews. Don't worry, my boy, you will. Michael is sure of it. But some Seniors never get it. And, some only get it after they've been a Senior for many years. Being named a full-fledged Senior doesn't automatically bring the privilege of going Below. It's just that *when* this technique is mastered it comes in handy sometimes so as to better serve your One Below," explained Marco. "Oh yeah, it is a prerequisite for being an Advanced though."

"What is it anyway? I don't even know what it is yet."

"TANAHI...or Temporary Apparent Non Association Human Intervention....well, it's exactly what its name suggests...temporary...apparent...non association...human...intervention. See, it's easy really once you break it down," Marco explained.

"Yes, I figured that, but what does it *mean?*"

Marco looked Below. "Hmmm, I do have about four or five minutes before I have to go down I think, so I suppose a crash course won't hurt any. Very well..."

Doc was fascinated. Marco was about to go Below...something that not every Guardian Angel did or might ever do. This was a chance to really learn something.

"Very well, for starters," Marco began his lecture, "and as you know, we Guardians are forbidden to go Below to interact with our assignments or to communicate directly with them....except in the most rarest of circumstances, going Below simply isn't an option 99 times out of 100. And don't forget very few of us know *how* to go Below properly—there's a proper way and an improper way, as the risk of error or being found out is great when we change levels of consciousness—so it is hardly ever employed. But, from time to time, it does come in handy," Marco said smiling as he peered downward and leaned over the railing running along the back row of the outside portion of the Gallery where he and Doc were sitting. Marco was watching intently for his opportune moment to go Below.

"So, yes, the first thing you should know about this technique is that it involves us going Below. Of course, that's not reflected in the name…it's a given. Next, as you can probably guess, our involvement Below is only temporary…hence the first word in the name… Temporary."

"Gotcha," said Doc.

Marco was still watching his assignment Below. "It's Apparent because our presence is apparent to those Below, but not as Guardian Angels, rather as…wait for it now…regular people. So, starting from the beginning we have Temporary—because it's not permanent— Apparent—because our presence is apparent to those Below, that is, we blend right into the crowd, as it were, and no one takes us for being what we really are—Guardian Angels. There…there are your first two components," Marco said as he was watching more keenly now the goings on that concerned him Below. "Are you with me?"

"Totally."

"Ok, good, the Non Association part comes in because when we are fulfilling our task Below we can't directly contact our assignment *per se*. In other words, we can't tell them who we are. We basically have to help by…Non Association. They have no idea who we are even though we could be standing right next to them. Oh yes, one more thing, it's very important not to come into physical contact with anyone when you're Below—that is, touch them or the like. That would be disastrous. 'Member what I said about the risks involved and the room for error is high?" Marco asked looking at Doc.

"Yes, I remember," Doc replied.

"Well, that's the reason. You can't touch anyone. The procedure would come crashing down with possibly some serious mental health issues being visited on the one you touched, and quite possibly death or serious physical injuries being visited on the Guardian and the person. At least, that's what the texts say. Something to do with too much energy being passed to the one Below. I really don't know for sure because I don't think anyone has failed during this technique yet, because only the best understand it and only the best ever get a chance to perform it," explained Marco. "Wait…I have to go…the opportune moment has arrived…I gotta go Doc," Marco said as he got up out of his chair and vanished over the railing in a swoop. "Watch and learn, my boy," said a voice in thin air.

"Ok, I'm watching," Doc said to the air around him. But he could see nothing. Nothing. No sign of Marco at all. Doc could hardly contain himself.

In the next instant Doc felt a huge gust of breeze come blowing in where he sat and the empty spot next to him. Doc turned to his left just for a moment to pick up his ball cap that had blown on the floor. He had just put it back on his head backwards—the way he always wore his cap—when out of nowhere he saw Marco sitting in his spot again.

Doc was impressed. "Wow! Done already? That was quick, I didn't even see anything."

"Hardly," said Marco as he went back to intently watching his concerns Below. "It was a false alarm. The opportune moment wasn't there yet. I thought it was, but it wasn't. Good thing I hadn't passed the point of no return yet, otherwise it wouldn't have gone quite to plan. You see, you have to be alive to all sorts of unexpectancies or changes as they're occurring in real time. Otherwise, all bets are off. See, only the Guardian Angels who are adept at picking up on signs and interpreting them are able to perform such a technique. Takes years of practice. Patience, too. But right now…I'd say I have about two to three minutes before showtime—for real."

Doc was ecstatic. He couldn't believe that he was actually going to see Marco go down Below and help his assignment in some way. Marco said something that made Doc think about something else he and Michael had spoke of. Michael said that Seekers were adept at picking up signs from their Guardian Angels to help them on their personal path. Now, he knew that great Guardian Angels also had to be adept at reading signs and being patient. Doc looked in awe at Marco whose gaze was intently fixed Below.

"Alright, so where was I?" asked Marco.

"You just explained Non Association," said Doc rather quickly, wanting Marco to finish his explanation before he had to leave again.

"Yes, right you are…next is Human. Human, for two reasons. One, because we take on the form of humans when we're down there; and two, because it's as humans that we do whatever it is we're trying to accomplish. Guarding, protecting, guiding, teaching or whatever. So, we have to do it in such a way that any human could do it. Whatever it is we are about to do, it must be done in such a way that it be seen as something a regular person would be capable of doing. Nothing about it can be celestial or extraordinary. It almost has to be seamless in its execution and simplistic in its operation. No one can suspect that it's not really a person doing the deed. Almost unnoticeable and unremarkable, if you get my meaning."

"I do…I do," said Doc enthusiastically.

"And, finally, Intervention. Intervention, because that's what we're doing. We're intervening in some way or other."

"Sooooo…we're helping our assignment Below on a temporary basis…whereby our presence is apparent to others…yet we cannot associate with anyone or tell them who we are, hence the Non Association…and we do it in a completely human fashion…if you do all that, the intervention is successful. There, TANAHI—Temporary Apparent Non Association Human Intervention. Clear?" Marco asked Doc.

"Inescapably," replied Doc.

"It's used when rolling out a garbage can—or whatever—from up Here, just won't do," Marco said very nonchalantly. "Ok, now I really gotta go…watch!" Marco said, as he vanished for the second time.

Doc watched but there was still no sign of Marco. Well, that makes sense, thought Doc, because if he's blending in Below I really don't know what he's supposed to look like.

Doc keyed in on the scene Below that Marco had been watching.

All Doc could see was an elderly woman passenger at the check-in desk at an airport talking to another lady—the check-in lady, an elderly woman behind the check-in counter at a small-town airport.

"I'm sorry, ma'am," said the disheveled check-in lady. It was her first day on the job and she knew the importance of following rules. "Rules are rules and you have to be here and checked-in forty-five minutes before a domestic flight. It is now...thirty minutes before the scheduled take-off."

"But I *was* here forty-five minutes before...your clock must be wrong. Besides nobody was behind the counter a few minutes ago," said the elderly woman passenger pleading her case. "You don't understand, I *have* to get on that flight."

They both looked up at the huge clock behind the counter. The huge hands read 10:30 on the huge face. The flight was leaving at 11:00. The check-in lady started punching numbers into her computer and finally said in an exasperated voice, "Oh, just wait a minute I'll see what I can do." It seemed that the check-in lady really didn't have a clue how to run the computer. "But don't trust a hope."

The elderly woman was just about to raise her voice and take her issue further, but she could see that doing that would get her nowhere. Especially now that there was a young man standing next to her who wanted to talk to the check-in lady.

"Hi...one adult for the eleven o'clock flight please," said the young man to the check-in lady who had her head down typing stuff into her computer. When she saw the man in front of her she almost jumped out of her skin. It was as if he appeared out of nowhere.

"I'm sorry sir, you have missed the check-in time. I'm dealing with this lady at the moment."

"Nooo," started the young man, "I *was* here forty-five minutes before the flight. I was trying to use the quick check-in kiosk right over there. For some reason, it wasn't working, so I thought that you could check me in manually."

"Sir, you weren't at the check-in kiosk," said the check-in lady, who looked over at the kiosk not ten feet from the front of the counter. "No one was standing there...you just walked up now."

Good old Marco, Doc thought, as he marvelled at how Marco

had transformed himself into this late-arriving young male. It was quite something. Marco wore a distinguished-looking goatee with very short hair while this young man had a full head of unruly locks and was clean shaven.

The elderly lady who was first refused a seat was slowly starting to feel better. Perhaps now that the check-in lady had *two* customers waiting to board, she might change her mind. The elderly lady passenger looked back at the kiosk. It *was* a mere few paces from the front of the counter. She hadn't seen anyone standing there before either.

If the young man *was* standing there trying to check in before the cut-off time, then by rights the check-in lady would have to let him through, thought the elderly woman. Then, if that was the case, she would probably have to let her through as well.

Realizing her predicament, the disheveled check-in lady radioed up to the gate to tell them that she had two more passengers coming. She started processing the elderly woman first. When that was done, she started to process the young man. "When I go through security, I'll tell them you're right behind me...I'll make sure they don't leave without you,' said the elderly woman, thankful that the young man happened along.

The elderly lady went through security but something in her bag set the alarm off on the x-ray belt. "Mind if we have a look in your bag, ma'am?" asked the security officer. "Not at all...go right ahead," said the elderly woman. The security officer started looking through the elderly woman's bag. By this time, the young man was checked and waived through by the security officers. He was now going up the escalators towards the departure gate.

After a brief moment, not finding anything of note in the elderly woman's bag, the security officer motioned her through. As she was leaving the security area and was about to get on the escalator, she saw the young man get off the escalator at the top and start towards the gate. Seconds later she had reached the top and was running towards the gate.

The hallway towards the gate was curved as it made its way to the departure area. The long curve prevented the lady from seeing any farther than about fifty feet in front of her at any given time. She wanted to thank the young man for helping her get on the flight, but by the time she got to the boarding attendant the young man was not in sight.

"You're the last one," said the boarding attendant. "You're lucky. The Captain had finished his pre-flight check and was just about to pull away from the gate. Passport…ok,…boarding pass…looks good…alright, you're all set to go. Enjoy your flight!" When the lady heard the boarding attendant say that she was the last one, she figured that the young man was already on the plane.

Right at that moment Doc felt a huge gust of wind and, Bam! there was Marco sitting next to him in the Gallery. "Whew, just in the nick of time. That was fun," said Marco. "So, whatd'ya think?"

Doc looked at Marco. He looked back down at the airport. Back to Marco. Back to the airport. Speechless he was. "Wha…how…I thought you…you're here," Doc said in astonishment.

"Of course I'm here," said Marco. "Where did you want me to be?"

"I don't know, it's just I thought that you were Below."

"I was…and now I'm here… *Temporary*…remember."

"Yeah, I guess so," replied Doc. "By the way, you do a young man perfectly."

"Young man?"

"Yeah, when you came out of nowhere and told her that story that you had been at the kiosk all along…that was great."

"Young man? You mean that guy with the brown mane? Doc…I wasn't the young guy…I was the check-in lady," Marco said under his breath for fear that he would get teased by the others in the Gallery.

"The check-in lady? Uh-uh. No way."

"Uh…yeah… *way*," said Marco. "You don't think in today's day and age with airport security being as tight as it is, they would bend the rules for anybody do you? Anyway, the regular check-in lady had just left her post because it was past check-in time so there was no more reason to have a person at the check-in counter. That's when I swooped in. If someone had been there, I would have had to have made different arrangements. But as it turned out, it worked out perfectly."

"But the young man…he appeared out of nowhere," Doc said in disbelief.

"Tell me about it…I have no idea where he came from," said Marco shaking his head. "That's why I nearly jumped out of my skin. Talk about change of plans. Heck, I didn't even know if they had one empty seat on the plane let alone two. Have you ever tried to figure out an airline booking system, huh? And me, with no computer experience. When I was growing up Below we counted with beads and sticks. Anyway, I was just having a little fun with him. Actually, I was focused on the computer trying to figure out how to check the elderly lady in the whole time. So I guess my Intervention ended up helping both of them…all the better. Good thing for the kid that the elderly woman had me in tow."

"Well, regardless, that was very well done Marco," said Doc. "I had no idea you were the check-in lady."

"Who knows Doc…well, God and Michael know, they seem to know everything, but besides them, who knows, you might grow up to be a lady one day," said Marco laughing.

Doc failed to find the humour. "Yeah…I guess…although I'm not sure if I could pull the lady thing off for my first intervention. Anyway, I gotta get going, I start my third Observational Period tomorrow. Thanks for the lesson. That was great."

"My pleasure, anytime," replied Marco. "You coming here to the Gallery to start your next Period?"

"No, I don't think so. It's fun, and I do learn a lot…but I think I need a little quiet time. I'll see you after though…and the rest of the clowns," said Doc pointing to the tomfoolery that was going on at the other end of the Gallery. As he got up to leave, he saw a chipmunk run off to the side of the raised platform where the two of them had been sitting at the railing. "Hey, look, there's Edmund."

Marco looked at the chipmunk. "That's not Edmund...that's Bandit. Can't you tell them apart?"

Doc couldn't. "Uh, not really...they kind of all look the same to me."

"Don't worry, like anything else, you'll get it in time," Marco said kindly.

"I 'spose," replied Doc as he waved goodbye to Marco. "See you later."

"Yup, later Doc...good luck with the rest of your Interviews. I'm here if you need me...I know sometimes Michael can be confusing," offered Marco.

"You're not kidding. Thanks, I'll keep that in mind...see ya," Doc said as he walked away from the Gallery.

16

---

tHe CORRIDOR of tHe saInts

Back at home Doc took out his notes and texts again. He decided to go over his material once more before he embarked on his third Observational Period the next day. Going over the various subjects slowly, Doc understood what the new concepts were he would need to employ Below and how they fit together.

It was really all about understanding how life worked, he thought. If I can understand things like patience, death and why things happen, then I really will be able to make a difference in the life of my One Below. Once I understand those things then all I have to do is communicate that understanding. I guess I'll do that by sending signs. Then over time, it will be up to my One Below to pick up on those signs—and listen to them—and use them advantageously. But how do I do that if I can't go down Below? I know TANAHI is only used once in awhile and even so, I don't think that is the method meant to be used for guiding, teaching and protecting day in and day out. This silent communication bit is a lot more difficult than playing with traffic.

Eager to learn more, Doc went back to his notes.

Patience…got it covered, he said to himself. Death, classification of people and how they chose to live their life…check, check. TANAHI…I know that too….*now*, he said to himself with a laugh. Michael will be pleased that I know what that is.

Finally, Doc came to a concept that he hadn't figured out yet, nor had talked about it in depth with Michael: The Parchment. God's Parchment. All Guardian Angels were told of The Parchment when they were in Basic, but as a Basic they really had no need to know what was contained on It, nor how it affected Guardian Angels. After all, a Basic Guardian Angel's job was simply to protect. They were not ready yet for talk of God's Parchment. All they were taught as a Basic was that it contained names of people Below and other information about them. Michael had told him that in time he would undoubtedly get to see The Parchment—Doc figured that time was now.

He knew that there was a copy in the Great Library Hall in the Academy and it was there for all Senior Guardian Angels—and higher—to view. He knew that anybody could walk in and use the First Library Hall, that is, the main part of the Library, during business hours, but only Seniors and above had access to the Great Library Hall—where a copy of The Parchment was kept. It was just after supper, so Doc decided to make the short walk to the Academy and have a look at The Parchment and see what was on it.

Doc shut the gate as he exited his little fenced-in yard in front of his house. As he clasped the gate shut, he looked down at the row of daisies that lined his waist-high fence.

I'd better get weeding that little bit soon or I'll have a great crop of chickweed instead of daisies, Doc thought, as stepped on the tiny path that meandered in front of his house. From the tiny path that meandered by his front yard, Doc forked right after a few hundred metres onto a slightly larger path. Then, he forked left till it met with a bigger path. Another fork right, then left. Finally, Doc rounded the sweeping curve at the end of this last path until it met up with The Main Path—the path that led right to the front doors of the Academy.

As it was dusk, Doc didn't see much activity on the Academy's grounds. Other than the odd Angel bustling along in the shadows, the accompanying breeze and a few woodpeckers, things were fairly quiet.

The Main Path ended—or started—at the front entrance of the Academy, as it was generally called. That is, The New Academy, where Doc wrote his final Junior exams and attended Senior Theory classes. The Old Academy was a few paths over, behind The New Academy. Mostly, The Old Academy was reserved for meetings of The Inner Circle. The New Academy was very, very new. It was only 2,000 years old and looked as if it was built yesterday. Pristine in its cleanliness; powerful in it's beauty.

The Main Path seamlessly turned into one big, flat, open, cobble-stoned space—perfect for gatherings—that led right up to massive stone steps, which in turn led to the colossal front doors. Anyone entering The New Academy would not be able to avert their eyes from the huge inscription above the doors: "Mark 10:27."

Doc, as he did every time he ascended the stone stairs, read the inscription and put it in his own words: "With men it is impossible, but not with God; for all things are possible with God." That inscription always gave Doc inspiration and hope when things weren't going right. Reading that made things go right. Doc had a knack for getting things to go right.

Looking up, just before he opened the front doors, Doc mouthed silently to the inscription, "Yes, they are. Thank You."

The two huge, ten-metre high, oak front doors with two-tonne black iron hinges—doors that were dwarfed ten-fold by the Academy itself—didn't creak or shudder as Doc opened them, giving way to the splendour of Pilate's Foyer. The doors opened as if they were light as feathers. Even though he had walked through those doors hundreds of times over the years, he always felt a sense of awe and humility each time. This time was no different.

This huge first room—Pilate's Foyer—had over fifty doorways and halls leading to other parts of the building. On the ceiling, 100 metres above the marble floor, was a mural of Pilate speaking to the throng on The Friday. Etched in the stone wall under the mural was the inscription, 'Take Him yourselves as I find no fault in Him.'

After Doc shut the Foyer's outer doors behind him, Doc walked towards the Great Library Hall.

To get there, Doc first went straight, bypassing all twenty-five doors on either side of the Foyer until it joined The Corridor of the Saints. This Corridor was hundreds of metres long and had portraits and statues of all the Saints and the seven Archangels. Some just had a portrait, others a statue. The great ones had both.

The Archangels were at the end of the Hall. Even though Michael was considered *the* Archangel, leader of his Order, closest to God and Heaven's greatest defender, the other six lesser members of the Archangel Order also had portraits in The Corridor: Gabriel, Raphael, Uriel, Sariel and Raguel. The sixth portrait, that of the fallen one, hung shrouded in darkness under a black, cast iron cloak. No number of legions could remove it. Doc felt a tingling go up his spine as he walked by. He quickened his pace until he got right to the end of The Corridor.

There was Michael.

Michael had both a portrait and a statue. His portrait and statue lay on either side of the open archway at the rear of The Corridor leading into The Himin Place—a great, tiled meeting place where students, professors, tourists and passers-by could meet for company, friendship and conversation. Above Michael's portrait read the words, 'The Great Prince—Leader of the Celestial Armies' and at the base of his statue were the words, 'He Who is Like God.' Both depicted the Archangel with his fiery sword. All great defenders had swords.

Doc was speechless as he gazed at Michael's likeness. Just like he always was when he had walked by Michael's portrait and statue on his way to Senior Theory classes. Remembering the first day they met at their bench, Doc now knew he had the greatest of teachers.

Just before entering The Himin Place, as Doc left The Corridor, he took one last peak at the words above Michael's portrait and substituted his own: 'Michael—The Great Rock Star and Victor of The Final Battle of the Bands.' Doc chuckled.

17

the parchment

The Himin was relatively round in shape, topped by a dome and had more windows than walls. The entire Place—floor, dome and walls—was adorned in the finest of marble and gold. On either side of The Himin were two smaller archways, each leading into smaller dimly lit corridors. Doc walked to the one on the left. The one on the right led to the classrooms. As Doc took the corridor that led to the library halls, he glanced quickly at the other corridor that led to the classrooms. Maybe I'll be back and visit you someday for my Advanced classes, he thought, as he ventured off towards to where The Parchment was kept.

Further down that dimly lit corridor on the right, about one hundred feet, was a set of regular-sized double doors—the entrance to the First Library Hall. Doc opened them and walked easily down the centre aisle amongst the small stacks of books. Doc was familiar with the First Library and knew where every subject was kept. He had spent many hours there during his Junior final exams and his Senior Theory classes.

Doc kept walking towards the back of the room. About halfway down the centre aisle he started to make out shapes on the back wall. Slowly, he could discern one very small door, straight ahead of him, on the back wall at the end of the aisle. He also made out a chair leaning up against the wall just to the left of the door. Doc was of average height, but he would have to stoop a little to get through the lone door.

The small, lone door led to the Great Library Hall and the chair was the night watchman's perch. The Great Library Keeper was almost asleep on his chair.

Dozing in and out of consciousness, but balanced perfectly on the two hind legs of his chair and the wall behind him, the Keeper almost fell off the back of his chair when Doc approached. He quickly shifted his weight forward putting him back on the chair's four legs and on solid ground.

"'Evening, son," said the Keeper, a little sleepily. "You looking to use the Great Library?"

"Yes sir," said Doc, "if I may."

"You may, if your name is on the list…and that might be…?" The Keeper had a list of all Seniors and higher who had special access to the Great Library Hall.

"Doc…Senior," replied Doc.

The Keeper ran his finger down the list "…Doc, Doc, Doc…ah yes, here it is," he said as he quickly looked up at Doc. "Says here… 'Doc, Senior *Candidate*.'"

"Yes, that's me."

"Sorry, son, only fully-fledged Seniors who have passed their Interviews have access."

"But I won't be long…I just want…"

"Wait a second, sorry, sorry, my mistake," the Keeper said quickly. "I should have kept reading. There's a little notation off to the right after 'Doc, Senior Candidate' that says, 'to enjoy full access *and* courtesy. M.' Hmmm, well, I guess you can go in. And since it says 'courtesy' may I bring you a drink or the like for your study period?"

The Keeper looked at Doc in a strange manner as if he was trying to figure out why this *Senior Candidate* was to enjoy courtesy, which meant refreshments, as well as access. Technically, only Advanced Guardian Angels enjoyed courtesy. Doc took a quick peak at the list and noticed the letter 'M' after the added notation. Good old Michael.

"No thanks…but thank you anyway…er…," Doc paused, wanting to address the Keeper by name but not knowing it.

"Oh…sorry. Woody. Nice to meet you."

"Likewise. No, but thanks again though. I won't be long," Doc said just before the entered the Hall.

"Anything in particular that you're looking for?" Woody asked Doc.

"The Parchment."

"Ah, yes, I think there's a copy of one already down on the first table up a ways on your right."

"Thanks…I won't be long."

Woody shut the door behind him after Doc made it through the doors.

After stooping down about a foot to get in, Doc was now, for the first time, in The Great Library Hall. The small doors were deceiving. After straightening up, and allowing his eyes to adjust to the little light thrown off by the odd candle, Doc looked around in amazement. The Great Library Hall was nothing like The First Library Hall. Here, the books seemed bigger—though it was hard to tell how much bigger without better lighting. The stacks seemed bigger and from Doc's first glance there seemed to be more books here than in the other library. And there was something else about this library, but Doc could not put his finger on it. Somehow, it felt different.

Remembering Woody say there was a copy of The Parchment

already on one of the reading tables, Doc started looking for it right away. He knew, or at least was told in Basic, that it was a book—of sorts. As he neared the table he made out an outline of a huge book sitting atop the table.

Here it is, thought Doc, as he edged closer. The Parchment was on a big cherry table right where Woody thought it was. The table sat by itself in a wide-open space as if it was the only object in a big clearing in the middle of a forest amid all the trees of books.

The Parchment, Doc found out, was a huge leather-bound book. It lay open roughly in the middle. Doc guessed it was perhaps a little over three feet long or high if it was standing on its end. From the spine to the outer edge of the pages he figured it would be about two feet wide when closed; four feet wide when opened and laid flat on its covers. When closed, it seemed to be over a foot in thickness from cover to cover.

It consisted of thousands upon thousands of pages. The lettering was black and very ornate. He was spellbound—he had never seen such a beautiful book before. And to think, Doc thought, God Himself wrote it. After all, it was God's Parchment. Doc pulled up a chair and started reading The Parchment.

The Parchment was laid open presumably where the last Guardian Angel was looking. Each page consisted of vertical columns—four columns on the left page, four on the right. He noticed that on the centre of each page, right at the top above the column headings, was printed today's date. He turned to a few other pages. Same thing. At the top of each page, above the columns, was today's date. Doc started looking at the columns; he started on the left-hand side.

The first column consisted of names of people Below; from top to bottom and on every page from front to back. The names were in alphabetical order. There must be hundreds of thousands of names in this book, thought Doc. The Parchment was open on a portion of the Bs. There were names written in English, Ukrainian, Arabic, Herero, and every other language imaginable.

To the right of that column was the second column that listed—

on the same corresponding line as their name—the person's date of birth. Next to that column on the right was a column titled Belief Date. Doc noticed that some of the dates in this column were in the past; and some entries displayed dates that had yet to come.

The fourth column had the heading of Current Classification. Doc quickly looked down that column. He saw the words Blamer, Exister and Content many times over. He didn't see the word Seeker. He turned the page again and again—still no Seeker. He flipped back to the page he started with.

The next column to the right of the fourth column—the fifth column and fourth from last—was a column titled End Classification. Doc noticed that many people had the same entry for their Current Classification as their End Classification. Lots of names had Blamer in both columns. Some had Exister entered in both. However, others had Exister under Current Classification but then had Content written under their End Classification. Hmm, Doc thought silently, seems like those people started out as Existers but at some point before the end they appear to become one of the Content. Good for them.

Doc looked for a Seeker. He started skimming more pages. Finally, he saw the entry Seeker under the End Classification column for somebody. He looked just to the left to see what the fellow's Current Classification was: Exister. "Wow!" exclaimed Doc. "Seems like this person really changed their life around. Great for them."

The column to the right of that column, the sixth column and third from last, had the title of G.A. and Rank. Doc looked down that column and saw the names of all the Guardian Angels who had guardianship over someone Below. Doc recognized the names of many of his friends. Now he knew that all types of people, whether they be Blamers, Existers, the Content or Seekers, had Guardian Angels. Some had Basic, others Junior; some had Seniors, others Advanced.

Doc realized the person's classification Below wasn't the defining quality as to whether they had a Guardian Angel assigned to them but rather it was their belief in God that determined whether they were given one. Just like the way Michael said it was, thought Doc.

The seventh and second-to-last column was titled Destiny Accomplished. The entry in this column was either a check mark or a blank. Some Blamers had the check mark; others didn't. Same thing for Existers, the Content and Seekers—some appeared to have accomplished their life's destiny; others hadn't yet. So, by looking at that column, Doc thought, I can figure out if a particular person Below has accomplished in life what it is meant for him to accomplish...but it tells me nothing of what that accomplishment is. It tells me nothing of whether this person Below is going to be a rock star, feed miller, chef, shoemaker or an excellent parent. Doc noticed that some Existers had a check mark under their Destiny Accomplished column. "I guess Michael was right," Doc said aloud, "maybe it is someone's life destiny to live out their days beholden to debt and stuff and to be unhappy...how depressing...especially when it takes no brains, skill or special education to be happy or to follow your inner desires. But maybe they have no inner desires." Doc shook his head in disbelief.

The eighth and last column was titled Death Date. Some lines were blank; others had dates. And, only dates that had passed were written in for someone who had, obviously, died. Hmmm, Doc thought, when someone passes away, the date is entered...but it appears that everybody who doesn't have a date listed is still alive. Unlike Belief Date where a date in the future might very well be entered on the Parchment, no date was entered under Death Date if the death hadn't occurred yet. For some reason, he thought, God doesn't want any of his Guardian Angels to know when their assignments are going to eventually die.

Doc was slowly piecing together the meaning of all the columns. It painted a picture, as it were, of the life-story of that person Below. Doc figured that each entry for each person Below was a like a snapshot in time of where that person was in their life. Kind of like a progress report. All those snapshots together painted a live, word-like picture.

The Parchment listed the person's name and birthdate. That's simple enough thought Doc. Then it has Belief Date—obviously denoting when that person Below started to believe in God and thus the date that a Guardian Angel would be assigned to that person—if the person was old enough to understand the concept of God—even if only on a rudimentary basis. Every entry in the Parchment had a Belief Date. Doc guessed that this was where all the believers were listed. Perhaps the non-believers were listed elsewhere, he supposed.

Next came the Current Classification column. On that particular day, it showed what classification the person Below was. The current date was displayed at the top of each page so Doc guessed that the Parchment must be updated daily as classifications change. That's a lot of updating, thought Doc. I wonder if Woody does that?

Doc figured that the End Classification was just that—what classification the person ended up as when they died.

The next column is easy enough to figure out, thought Doc. This just shows what Guardian Angel has guardianship over that particular person Below. But what Doc found interesting was that one classification of people Below had different ranks guarding them. Some Exister's had Juniors; some Content had Juniors. Some Seniors had those that were Content. One's classification didn't determine the rank of Guardian Angel that was assigned to them.

The Destiny Accomplished column was also easy to figure out, Doc surmised. Some Below had already reached their life's destiny; other's had not. Some Existers had reached their destiny; others had not. Some had appeared to already have reached it even though their End Classification was listed as an Exister. Gleaning information between the lines, Doc guessed that it was always open for people Below to change their lot in life if they wanted to. And, since this was God's Parchment, He already knew if they had reached it—even though their date of death might be some time far off.

In the last column—the Death Date column, Doc just figured that this was used as a record keeping function. Or maybe it could be used by someone's Guardian Angel to check into a death date of a friend or family member of someone who that Guardian Angel was guarding at the present. That could come in handy, thought Doc.

Doc read page after page. Hours went by. He marvelled at the different combinations of entries different people had. There didn't seem to be one set pattern. Some Blamers had reached their life destiny; other had not. Some Existers had Junior Guardian Angels; some of the Content had Juniors. Some of the Content had reached their destiny; others did not. Some, it appeared, would stay in the same category their whole life; others, it seemed, would improve their lot in life. Occasionally, as Doc noticed, some seemed to regress as they went from being Content as of today's date to being listed as a Blamer in their End Classification.

Eventually, as Doc tired, he decided it was time to go home. Pleased with himself that he had unlocked the meaning to the entries in The Parchment, Doc closed the book. On its cover and spine in a beautiful gold coloured font was the following silk inlay: "B: 578 of 13,074."

Doc was speechless. This huge leather book was number 578 of 13,074—of the Bs! This was only one book covering people Below with the surname starting with B out of 13,074. And there must be hundreds of thousands of names in each book, thought Doc.

Slowly, Doc lifted his head and looked more carefully at the stacks of books that bordered the open space where the table sat. Doc's eyes followed the stacks upward. And upward still. Doc could not see the top of any stack. They went up and up. And there were hundreds of stacks. Doc tried to look for the ceiling. He couldn't see one. The stacks reached upward as far as the eye could see.

That's what different...I can't see the ceiling, he said to himself, as he craned his neck in order to get a glimpse of where the top of the stacks was or where the walls ended and the ceiling began.

Each stack seemed to have no end and there were hundreds of stacks. And on each stack there were hundreds of Parchments. Doc walked over to the nearest stack closest to his table and put his hand on the railings of a movable ladder on a frame with wheels. Doc looked up. He couldn't see the top of the ladder.

Wanting to explore more, he went over to the wall and took a candle, hanging just above eye level, out of its holder. With candle in hand, Doc started to walk through the stacks beyond where his table was. This led him towards the back of the Great Library Hall. He saw many more stacks of books—or Parchments, as he had now figured out.

Walking still further towards the back of the Great Library Hall, Doc came across another table in the middle of an open space. No Parchment was on this table. He went to the stack closest to the table and read the printing on the spine of one particular Parchment: "C: 12,748 of 16,803."

Doc went further still. He finally came to the start of the Ds. As far as his eyes could see in the dim light were stacks and stacks of Parchments reaching up to the ceiling, wherever that was.

18

the talking hall

Doc was mesmerized. Imagine, the name of each believer Below is contained somewhere in these Parchments. I've never seen anything like it before. "How are all these Parchments updated daily?" Doc asked aloud to the empty Hall.

When the room answered, Doc almost hit the ceiling. "By God," uttered a voice behind him. As Doc spun around to face the empty room he dropped the candle. His knees went weak. He had to lean against a stack to keep his balance. With no light at head level Doc could not see who the answerer was. Trembling, Doc squinted as he tried to make out who was—or what—was with him in the empty hall—if anybody.

"Who else do you think updates them?" asked the voice. "Do you know how many entries there are? And never mind the entries, each page has the current date on it, which is also updated daily."

Doc still didn't speak. He couldn't. He left his tongue somewhere between his mouth and the ceiling. He still couldn't see who was talking. His eyes were hiding behind his brain. They had no desire to make out who the visitor was. Doc had never been so scared in his life—or his Angelic life.

The voice was that of a person. The person bent down and picked up the candle and brought it to his face. It was Woody. Doc's lungs were his first organ to rejoin him. He finally breathed a sigh of relief, thankful that it was a familiar face.

At exactly the same time—with Doc stammering and Woody wondering—they both asked the other if everything was alright.

"Sure everything is alright...it's past midnight you know...and you said you wouldn't be long...so after not seeing you come out after some time, I thought I would check up on you. When I got to the first table I saw the candle was gone, so I had nothing to light my way. I should have brought my candle from the door but I thought that...never mind...anyway, when I saw you weren't at the first table and the candle gone, I thought something might be wrong. But all's well that ends well...so everything is alright then?" asked Woody.

Still barely able to speak, Doc replied. "Yes, yes everything's fine. I just wanted to see how far back the stacks go...how far back *do* they go, Woody?" asked Doc.

"To the Z's," replied Woody with a puzzled look on his face. What kind of alphabet is this guy using? Woody wondered silently.

This of course wasn't Doc's meaning, but he didn't press. Doc was asking if The Parchments stretched all the way back to the faint, faint light coming from the back of the room. A light he could barely see that actually looked like a white glow of sorts which seemed to emit an omnipresent feeling of warmth that travelled right through Doc's bones.

Laughing nervously, Doc said, "Of course they go to the Zs...

what was I thinking? Well Woody, I think I'm done for the night, it's time for bed."

"Don't let me stop you," Woody said kindly. "I was just checking up on you, that's all. You're free to stay as long as you like."

"No, no, thanks. I found what I was after, thanks. Oh, maybe one more question after all…how *high* do the stacks go?"

Woody looked up. "To the ceiling…why, did you want them to go higher?"

"Nope, the ceiling is high enough I guess. Sounds good to me." Doc looked up again, but still couldn't see any ceiling.

Woody just shook his head. Maybe I should've brought this guy some courtesy. Like maybe a good, stiff Scotch or something. How high do the stacks go? What are they teaching these kids these days? He smiled politely at Doc.

They both walked back out of the dark rows of stacks towards the small door leading out of the Great Library Hall into the First Library Hall where Woody had his post. Quickly glancing up at the big clock above the door, Doc noticed that it was indeed after midnight. Wow, I was in there a long time.

Just after the pair exited the Great Library, Woody turned around, bolted the door and took his seat. "See ya around Doc," Woody said as he slowly sipped a steaming cup of coffee.

"Oh, for sure, I imagine I'll be back from time to time. Thanks again, Woody."

Woody didn't say anything…he just gave Doc a big wave and a smile as best he could with the coffee mug up to his lips.

And ease up a point or two off the rum, Woody, Doc said to himself as he returned the Keeper's wave. Smiling at Woody politely as he left, Doc figured that coffee wasn't the only thing in Woody's mug.

Doc walked back through the First Library Hall, out its double doors, down the small corridor, through The Himin Place, under the archway, past Michael, down The Corridor of the Saints, into Pilate's Foyer, out the large outer doors to the stone stairs and onto the Main Path. After a few forks and turns, Doc was home.

Tired, Doc needed some sleep. It would be a big day tomorrow—the start of the third Observational Period. And, his daisies needed weeding.

19

SHORELINE SILENCE

After his morning coffee at home and some quick daisy tending, Doc headed to where he would do his observing—at least the observing he was going to do that day: his favourite spot down on the shore of his favourite lake. The *only* lake as far as Doc was concerned. Not many people came to her shores. Just the way Doc—and the lake—liked it.

To Doc, the lake brought comfort, peace, guidance and conversation. It was as if the lake was alive and spoke to him. To Doc, she was alive. It was as if they dwelt as one. It was as if there was a special bond or connection between the two of them. Doc knew he felt it and he even thought his lake felt it too. An unspoken connection.

Doc always cleaned and tended to his favourite part of the shoreline and the lake always seemed to tend to Doc in return. It was if the lake brought Doc comfort in such a way as if she was saying "Thank you, Doc, for looking after my shores."

Doc did some of his best thinking there throughout his life as a Guardian Angel. Funny, he thought, how an inanimate thing such as a lake can bring me comfort and peace. When I talk to her, she talks back. She even brings me knowledge, helps me learn, helps me see through things. Not only guardianship problems, but sometimes just life problems. My lake must be a smart lake.

Thinking of learning, Doc went over in his mind all of the learning he had covered over the last little while. "That's a heck of a lot of new learning," Doc said to his lake. "I didn't know there would be so much."

He sat down on his favourite rock and reclined, smiling, because he was happy where he was at in his Angelic life. This is what Doc liked to do best. Be by himself and think. That was how he learned—but it also doubled as his entertainment of choice. The solitude brought him knowledge and it brought him his entertainment. Both brought him happiness.

"Hey," Doc said to his lake, "I just figured out what I'm going to be concentrating on during this Period." There was silence. The lake never answered out loud when they had their conversations, but she always, always spoke to him. "I'm going to see what everybody Below is doing for entertainment these days." There was more silence. Kind of a questioning silence. "Ok, well, entertainment other than reality T.V. and stuff, is that better?" said Doc in response to the knowing silence. The sun beamed off the water closest to the shoreline and reflected a glisten.

20

tHe ϛReat HeLPeR

During that first day of observing, Doc soon found out that it was awards week Below, as it were. Many of the entertainment industries and other media outlets just happened to be holding their awards banquets that week. There were the awards for actors, for musicians, for authors. There were still yet awards nights for person of the year for this town and that town. Awards for entrepreneurs and bravery. For teachers and for architects.

Night after night Doc observed these awards banquets.

Wow, there sure are some very successful people in all walks of life.

Some, as he found out during one of his morning reads of *BEN* where the previous nights winners were listed, were famous. Some were not. Some were known across the entire planet Below; some weren't known outside their small town. Some were millionaires; some were of very modest means. These winners came in all shapes and sizes.

Someone's life destiny can also come in all shapes and sizes I bet, thought Doc.

The awards that were being handed out were as diverse as the winners who won them. All of them had at least one quality—and Doc figured maybe more—that they shared with the others: they were highly successful in their chosen task or field.

However, that quality of success was predicated on something deeper—something from within. The winner of the Best Actor award shared at least one quality with the person who won Nurse of the Year at a small-town hospital: the determination to strive to be the best they could be. The winner of the Rock Band of the Year award shared that same determination with the winner of Best Girl-Guide Leader. These winners were not Existers, thought Doc.

As the week wore on and Doc watched more awards banquets, he made another connection. Many of the winners—whether they were heavy metal rockers or actors or community leaders—seemed to thank one person in particular in their thank you and acceptance speeches. This one person was in many—not all, but many—of the speeches.

Doc did a quick survey of all the acceptance speeches. While many of the winners thanked their mothers and fathers, each winner had a different mother and father. However, there was one person that was mentioned more often than any other. The person wasn't mentioned in *all* the speeches, but a good number of them.

The winner of the Best Rap Music award mentioned this person. The captain of the champion professional football team and all his teammates thanked the person. The coach did as well. The winner of the Best Actress award mentioned this person. Parent of the Month also mentioned this person. And, when they did make reference to the person, the reference was usually first.

God.

The same person that was thanked repeatedly by different people, from different backgrounds, with different lifestyles and different amounts of money, was God. Many of these people who were judged by their peers and critics to have excelled in their chosen field recognized God as being an important part of their success. Important enough to thank Him and even more important enough to thank Him first.

Many, many of the winners started out their acceptance speeches by saying that "I'd like to thank God because nothing is possible without Him."

Gee, Rapper and Rocker of the Year are right, thought Doc, all things do come from Him and anything is possible through Him. And is it ever nice to see these people recognizing God's good work in public.

He knew it was not a matter of chance that this same person was mentioned time and time again: they really believed in Him and all that He stood for.

The fact that these public figures were stating, in public, the positive effect God had in their lives was impressive to Doc. It's not advertising, he said to himself. It's not a paid promotional commercial. The winners aren't getting money for mentioning those who helped them—whether it be God, their mom or their producer. They are, quite simply, acknowledging their helpers. God is such a great helper.

I guess Michael was right again, thought Doc, as he remembered—yet again—one of the Archangel's statements where he said, *'God is always willing to let people—of all various states of existence—prove their worth, Below and up Here. He will always give you ample opportunity. It's up to you to seize it—wherever you are. You just have to believe in Him and believe in yourself.'*

Who knew that acceptance speeches could be so educational? Doc asked himself. He loved learning, especially from the unlikeliest of teachers.

Doc left his lake on the last day of his third Period and headed for home.

21

POWER IS RELATIVE

While walking the path home Doc felt his latest observations were important ones as he realized what many of the acceptance speeches were telling him. Some of the successful people Below were saying that their success was kind of like a team effort: them and God. Doc had a feeling that it was a team of three with him and other Guardian Angels fitting in there somewhere, but he was still trying to figure out the "where." Actually, he knew "where" he fit in; he just had to work out the "how."

With his third Observational Period over and his Interview with Michael the next day, Doc crawled into bed and reflected on some of those thank-you speeches and how, to him, it seemed like a team effort.

Doc figured that God wanted everyone Below to succeed—whether that be as a parent, a friend, a secretary, a rock star or a world leader. In short, thought Doc, God just wants everyone to succeed in life—whatever that path might be. God is the leader of the team and will present ample opportunity to everyone Below so they can seize it and live a meaningful life. All the people Below have to do is buy into the team and seize the opportunity.

Doc also guessed that the success God wanted each person Below to achieve could be viewed as being synonymous with happiness in some cases. God wanted everyone Below to be happy. But He did leave it up to them to realize that success, or happiness—or not. It was entirely up to them.

After thinking awhile Doc knew that it wasn't enough to just buy into God's existence in order to be successful because he remembered that people listed on The Parchment were believers yet some were destined to live their life out as Blamers or Existers beholden to stuff.

No, they *really* have to believe in Him—*really* buy into the team. When the people Below buy into the team, then great things can be accomplished…I just know it. If they *truly* buy into the greatness of the team…..then that person's life Below will henceforth soar to new heights. Maybe that's what is meant by the Pure Joy that Michael spoke of.

Doc turned his light out and kept thinking in the dark. "God," he said aloud to his empty, dark room, "already knows the power of the team. All people Below need do—well, one of the things they need do—to complete the team and see their life's destiny change from Exister to maybe a Seeker is believe in the power of God. From there, people Below will have found part of the equation that will unleash love, greatness and happiness.

"That's such a simple principle isn't it?" Doc asked his room. "Too bad it's being figured out by far too few people. Such a shame really because the answer is so simple. Believe."

Knowing that God was but one part—albeit the biggest part—of the equation to success and happiness, Doc set his mind to work on uncovering the other components of his solution.

God, as leader of the team, will always give the person Below the freedom to belong to the team or not. It is the person's choice whether they want to sign up. I guess the person Below is always, always the true author of their fortune or misfortune. The person Below has the final say in how they live their earthly life. They're the ones that have to give their life at least some direction; some chance of success. If they don't buy into the team, then the team, or rather God, is powerless. He can either be powerful or powerless and it is entirely up to the person Below. God is only as powerful as the person Below allows.

Doc thought that an amazing concept. God is all-powerful and powerless all in the same breath. God's power is relative.

He repeated it, only this time he said it aloud. "God is only as powerful as the person Below allows." He thought about the meaning of that before he moved on...

Doc started pondering his premise further.

I suppose, generally, God won't interfere with people's choices they've made as to how they want to live their life. I guess that's why there are criminals Below. They made a choice to live like that. Just like the winners of various awards; they decided to live their life *that* way. It seems to me that it all boils down to choices.

God gave people Below the ability to do anything—He gave them boundaries unknowable, Doc pointed out to himself.

If only people knew the true capacity of their mind...if they only knew the true power of their soul...if they only knew the true resiliency of their spirit, then, I think, some people might be able to improve their lot. And most importantly, He gave them the ability to *change*...The Parchment says so. And I know The Parchment is Truth. His Truth.

"The ability to change," said Doc, talking to himself, "there's another important point. I'll have to tell Michael about that one. But sometimes change is hard work. Sometimes change doesn't come overnight. Yes, most times it only comes through hard work."

"Change, like happiness, is hard work that comes over a period of time. A period of time that might have hardships. I guess that's where the belief in the team comes in handy. It's probably at those times when God carries more of the load and makes sure you stay on your road to positive change. I think Michael even said that once, something about once a person Below believes in Him, He will never let you down...or maybe he said that God would never betray you. And, somewhere, I come in with signs to help my assignment reach their destiny."

Doc figured that God really would come in and help with burdens Below at various times—whether those burdens were temptations or depression, or failure and rejection.

I think it says that in the Bible somewhere too, thought Doc, a little ashamed for not knowing exactly where it was. Where was that quotation? he asked himself again. Not having the citation on the tip of his tongue, Doc turned the light on and reached over and grabbed the Bible that was on his nightstand.

Now...where was that bit about temptation...yup, here it is, uh huh, right where I thought it was, said Doc silently only fooling himself. Ah yes, 1 Corinthians 10:13:

> No temptation has overtaken you but such as is common to man; and God is faithful, who will not allow you to be tempted beyond what you are able, but with the temptation He will provide the way of escape also, that you may be able to endure it...

...and so on and so forth. Doc's eyes were starting to close. He had had a good week of observing and his productive thought sessions did help him figure out how the concept of teamwork really did translate into good things for people Below.

"God helps those who help themselves," were Doc's last words before he fell fast asleep. He was ready to meet Michael for his next interview.

22

aLL thinGs are possiBLe

"You're late," Michael said, somewhat sternly but not too. Edmund, who was in the Archangel's right hand eating a mixture of seeds, rolled his eyes at Doc and then looked back at Michael as if to say, "What do you expect from a hotshot Senior Candidate?" Of course Doc was anything but; he was confident in his abilities yet completely comfortable with knowing when to ask for assistance.

"I am?" asked Doc apologetically. Michael's facial expression didn't change. "Yes, well, what do you know," Doc agreed even though he knew he wasn't and it was really the Archangel that was early, "…I am late. Sorry 'bout that."

It's best not to argue with the Archangel, especially when he was doing your Senior Interviews and had the ability to pass or fail you. Besides, Michael was touchy about stuff like that. Apparently, Archangels are never early. Nor are they late. They arrive precisely when they mean to. A Senior Candidate, on the other hand, could very well be late—even though he wasn't late at all—if it was the Archangel that had arrived early ahead of you and it was you that he was waiting on even though you were far from being late in the first place.

Michael looked at Doc following the circular reasoning going on in Doc's head. The Archangel started moving his head in circles trying to follow Doc's argument. He was getting dizzy.

"Enough!! Stop that!"

Doc knew Michael was following his thoughts and chuckled. He also knew what made the Archangel touchy. "What?! I'm not doing anything."

"Yes, you are. You're thinking you weren't really late if it was I who was early and if I was late then you'd be late and if you were late then the whole world would be early and if I was late then… ENOUGH!"

Doc's chuckle turned into an outright laugh.

Michael shook his head, flipping his locks out of his face. Geesh, I hate it when he does that.

"Aaaanyway," started Michael, "no worries, my boy…in fact, I might have been a touch early…which wouldn't make you late at all." Michael started laughing as he looked up at the sun trying to figure out the time and quickly forgot whether he was early or late or on time.

No kidding, Doc said to himself as he forced a thank-you smile.

"Oh and uh, sorry about not making it to see you after your second Observational Period…I was…uh…detained," said Michael apologetically. "I was hearing Freud's appeal from the Other Place. Seems now after all these years that he's been dead he really wants to be up Here now instead of There."

"So, yes, back to more important things…" said Michael as he started into the business at hand, "have you been busy? I'm sure you have lots to tell, don't you? How did your second and third Periods go? Have you learned anything? We haven't met for some time, have we?" Michael said as he started rubbing Edmund behind his ears.

Doc didn't know where to begin. He thought he had better start at start. "Well, I've…"

Michael cut in rather abruptly. "*Oh yes, you've been to the Gallery—haven't you?*" the Archangel said in a somewhat antagonistic tone. "And you got a few pointers on TANAHI on the side, *huh, huh, didn't you?* Oh and let's see, what else…you dropped a candle in the Great Library Hall and scared the wits out of Woody after midnight…"

Well, no, said Doc silently, actually it was Woody who scared me but…

Michael started up again before Doc could finish his thought.

"Never mind whose fault it was. And you took in all the awards shows Below, didn't you? Hmmm, must be nice to have time to Observe the *in-crowd*. You know, I never had time to Observe the *in-crowd* in my younger days. Nope, just me the Archangel, always trying to learn stuff. Fighting celestial battles. Defender of the Faith. Patron Saint of Ancient Mariners. Getting blisters on my hands from wielding Holy Swords…that were aflame. Boring little me. No time for entertainment. Tell me… tell me, did you find any time between the music and acting awards to do any learning? No, wait, I know, did you find anytime in there to do any *Bible study?*"

Oops, busted, thought Doc. But I guess he doesn't consider his jamming to Metallica and Pearl Jam as entertainment.

"Whatever you're thinking…don't. Just answer the questions."

How do I handle these allegations? I can get out of the Great Library Hall candle affair pretty easily enough…besides Michael had a hunch I was going to go and have a look at The Parchment because he even told Woody to extend me 'courtesy.' And he'll be happy with the connection I made between the awards shows and God and the teamwork involved. So there's two down. I suppose I'll just refer to my experience with Marco at the Gallery as me taking an active role in continuing my education. Now, how do I spin the fact that I wasn't up on my Bible? That one might prove the hardest. Confound you Michael, for knowing everything!

"I'm waaaiting…Doc, Senior *Candidate*," Michael said as he rolled his eyes at Edmund with Edmund returning the roll. "Wellll…?"

Doc knew Michael made mountains out of molehills. Probably something about being more impressive to move. This little episode was just the same as his little meltdown he had when they first met. Doc knew that Michael wasn't really mad. It was just his way—his funny, weird way.

"*Wellll?*" Michael said again waiting for Doc's answers.

"I'm waiting," said Doc.

"Yes, well, that's great dude, but so am I," replied Michael. "I'm waiting for some answe….waaait a minute, what are *you* waiting for, young man? *I'm* the only one waiting here. I'd like to know…"

Doc cut in, kindly. "I'm waiting for a few moments to pass so as to help ease your displeasure," Doc said in the best aristocratic enunciation he could muster. "After all, delay is the best remedy for anger." Doc smiled. Edmund cracked a smile. After a moment or two, Michael grinned as well.

"Ok, Mr. Awards Shows," Michael said playfully, "how's about you fill in the blanks for me. I already know what you did and saw—remember, I'm the Archangel—but humour me, what did you *learn* in your last two Periods?"

"Michael…," Doc said very proudly, "they went great…really. I learned so much."

Michael was pleased. He knew Doc would not disappoint. They both slouched back on the bench and reclined under the warm, clear breeze. Before Edmund was finished packing the last few seeds into his cheeks from out of Michael's hand and had departed for his hole, both Angels were in deep discussion.

Doc started the debriefing in earnest. "Well, for starters, I've learned that by and large, and in general, there are four types of people Below: Blamers, Existers, the Content and Seekers. I figured that one out on my own, but confirmed it in the Great Library."

"Hmmm…I see…continue."

"Basically, the categories reflect—and again, it's only a generalization, but a solid one nonetheless—the way people live their lives. Blamers have become accustomed to blaming others for their woes or misfortunes. For them, it's far easier to blame someone for their lot in life than it is to work hard to try and overcome those misfortunes. It's also easier to blame someone else for their unhappiness than it is to work on making themselves happy—to experience happiness. The majority of Blamers do so on account of their own free will because God has given each person Below the freedom to live their life any way they see fit. If they want to blame others for how their life has unfolded, then so be it—they are completely free to do so. Most of them don't care to find out what their life destiny might be because they're too busy blaming others for the past instead of concentrating on the future."

"Do any of these Blamers believe in God?" asked Michael.

"Sure, they can if they choose. Being a Blamer or Seeker or what have you is not predicated on their belief. Anybody is free to believe in God regardless of how they choose to live their life. Of course, most Blamers *really* haven't bought into God's existence. They might believe in His existence, but that's about it. Otherwise, if they really bought into His existence then they probably wouldn't blame so much. They would probably be one of the Content or maybe even a Seeker. A Blamer might believe in God but that person has yet to unlock the true power and message of God."

"So what quality is it that is common amongst Blamers?" Michael asked, pleased with Doc's finding so far.

"Unhappiness. Unhappiness, that's rooted in the past. Their present is always rooted to the past. They never look out into the horizon and realize that there is no unhappiness yet in the future because it has yet to come to pass. They just *think* the future will bring unhappiness because that's all they've experienced. You see, their future, to them, is their past. It's like they're engineering, at present, their future, based on the past. They never realize that the happiness they *could* work toward in the future is a real possibility because they're too busy living the present through events that have already taken place. They have resigned themselves to foreclosing on the future, based on the life they've lived heretofore. They never get to see the future because they never *truly* live it. Their present is always the past; their future is always the present…which brings them back to the past. Michael, it's an awful vicious circle they've gotten themselves into."

"That's the first bit of logical reasoning you've come up with that makes sense. Complete sense. And, by the way…you're right. Now, you mentioned Existers…tell me what you know of these people," prodded Michael.

"Well, they just exist. Many are beholden to things. To stuff. I've come to hate that word, Michael…'stuff.' Many people just exist their way through life in order to have stuff. Some of these Existers, because they're focusing on material things, get themselves into financial difficulties. Many are in debt. They want stuff. *And more stuff.* And they want it *now!* The fact that they can't afford it seems to have no bearing on the issue. They want it. They want it now. So they buy it—and quite often they go in debt to get it. Then the debt cycle starts…the debt cycle fuelled by the stuff cycle."

"Yes, I think we discussed this after your first Period," Michael reminded Doc. "And I remember saying that being beholden to stuff or just existing your way through life Below might in fact be their destiny in life. Do you agree with me now?" asked the Archangel, curious to see if Doc's views had changed.

"I guess if they continue to just exist without following their dreams then, yes, I agree. I agree that that obviously will be how they live out their days and in essence just existing during their life-time will be their life's destiny. But I know that some do not want to stay Existers. They want to change somehow to follow something else—something better; something greater. All Existers have the free-dom to change their lot in life if they want to; just like the Blamers. So for the ones that do change, I guess in those cases, then it won't be their destiny to live their life being beholden to credit card debt, no money down events and stuff."

"How do they do that?"

"Patience. Hard work. Maybe believing more forcefully in God. God works in mysterious ways and He really does help those that help themselves. Knowing that they *don't* have to resign themselves at the age of thirty-five to the fact that their current lot in life will continue forever if they don't want it to. Life's like a revolving door, Michael. Every once in a while, life will present you an opportunity to get out of your circular existence—and all they need do is take it. Or, they can keep walking right past those opportunities and stay inside their present, one-dimensional, revolving existence. Most choose to stay inside their circular existence without ever stepping out in order to see what great opportunities lie outside their revolving chamber. Of course, the big difference between a revolving door and life is the opportunity to get out and change your direction. In a revolving door, opportunity comes at regular intervals while life opportunities might not come so regularly or with the same frequency. When life opportunity comes you have to seize it."

"Are the Existers Below happy?" asked Michael.

"They could be, but usually not…for various reasons. One reason might be that their creative passions or dreams are being stifled by debt and they can't break their circular existence to get out of debt and really follow their dreams. Or, they might be unhappy for reasons that have nothing to do with debt. For whatever reason, they've come to the point that they are going to just exist because changing will simply entail too much hard work. Sometimes, like I said, it has nothing to do with debt. Sometimes people Below work at barely tolerable jobs that they would rather not have—yet they are very conscientious with their money and have no debt. Nonetheless, they are unhappy with their job and just figure that this will be their lot in life. Happy or not."

"Well then, is it not then their life destiny to live out their days being unhappy, but with no money problems?" asked Michael.

"Yes," said Doc very softly. "Yes, that will be their destiny."

"Do they believe in God?" asked the Archangel.

"Yes, some do…some don't. Yet how they believe in God is similar to how the Blamers believe: the belief isn't that forceful. After all, if you believed—and I mean *really* believed in God—then by operation of fact it would be almost impossible to be unhappy. Oh sure, everyone Below goes through their ups and downs at various times—I know I have—but to remain unhappy your entire lifetime is a sure sign that your belief in God isn't that strong. It can't be any other way. It's impossible. To believe in God from the deepest part of your soul is the quickest way to happiness. Now, happiness doesn't come overnight—just like success doesn't—but the surest way to realize happiness—longlasting and satisfying happiness—is to believe in God and all that He stands for."

"Alright, but what of the Content? What defines them? Are their lives like revolving doors?" asked Michael. In all his years Above, Michael had never heard a younger Angel refer to life that way. And slowly, Michael was beginning to realize that Doc wasn't a superstar or a hotshot. He was just Doc. Just a regular guy with no more brain matter than the next guy. He just *used* it. He also gave his soul a chance to speak. And he listened to it. Doc would make a fine Senior.

"What defines them?" Doc repeated. "Just that. They are the Content because they're content in their life Below. They're happy. They're happy where they are in their life and they like living just the way they're doing it. They're happy with their jobs, their family, their financial situation or what have you. For the most part, most of the Content do believe in God. However, like others in different classifications, they need not believe in God to be there. Some Content believe in God; others do not. But I would venture a guess that the happiness the believers experience is a deeper happiness than the non-believers experience…for the same reason I mentioned just a moment ago: a belief in God automatically brings one comfort, peace and happiness. And, if I may," added Doc wanting to say one more thing, "I would say that for the vast majority of them, they have found their destiny in life. That may be as a mechanic or a famous actor—it matters not. They've found their destiny because this is where most of them will live out their days. They are content to say that 'yes, this is my life and this is the way that it will end up.' It is satisfying to them."

"Well, Blamers can also say, can they not that, 'this is my destiny in life; this is my lot and I'm going to finish my days blaming people for the past without ever experiencing what might have been in the future'?" asked Michael.

"Absolutely. However, the difference is one of *happiness* and the degree and extent with which they believe in God."

"That's very good, Doc. However, the real test, as you know, has yet to come."

"Yeah...I know," replied Doc quietly. Doc knew that Michael would ask him what a Seeker was. He had a pretty good idea insofar that he figured they were people Below who kept striving to improve themselves, kept looking for their destiny in life. But Doc knew that there was still something missing in his answer. Because the Content could also look for their destiny in life without being a Seeker. There was still a defining quality—or qualities—that he had yet to uncover.

"Very well then," Michael said as began his next question, "what is..."

"TANAHI?" Doc asked, as he pre-empted the Archangel's imminent question on the qualities of a Seeker. "I never thought you'd ask Michael. Well, let me tell you..."

"Uh, that wasn't quite my question, but seeing as we do have to cover the subject that *you* raised, I suppose we could cover it now.... ok, what is it?"

Doc gave his definition and then summed it up nicely. "It's basically a fun way to help out your assignment Below—for only the most skilled Guardian Angels."

Michael pondered Doc's response. He had never heard it described in such a way. "Is it now? A *fun* way you said...oh, how so?"

"Well, it's fun," started Doc, with a sense of excitement similar to the excitement he felt when he watched Marco go Below, "...because you get to do down Below and be whatever you want. Kind of gives your level of consciousness up Here a break for a minute or two, if you get my meaning. Marco changed his appearance when he went Below."

"Did he now?" asked Michael with a look of skepticism. "What was he?"

"An elderly woman behind the check-in counter in the airport of a small town." Michael looked on without saying anything.

Doc kept going. "Yes, it appears to me that going Below for a temporary intervention can be great fun for us and helpful for our assignments Below. I know the risks are high so only those most adept at performing such acts will ever be able to carry it out. I also realize that it's only used rarely when, for one reason or another, we can't help from up Here. And really, Michael, those times will be rare," Doc said as if it was he who was doing the teaching. "...I know that. I guess it's just one more skill in the repertoire of really good Guardian Angels. I intend to master it one day. But I don't think I'm ready for it just yet. I'll get it."

"Oh, I have no doubt you will," replied Michael. "An elderly woman behind the check-in counter in the airport of a small town huh? Seems to me I need to have a little word with Marco. A woman, eh?"

"Yeah, he was great," Doc said, "he even had me fooled."

"I'm sure he did," Michael said shaking his head. "Leave it up to Marco to inject a little fun in this business. Sooo, I see you met Woody, eh...our Great Library Keeper?"

"Yeah...nice guy...even offered me a refreshment for my study period, he did."

"I also understand you saw The Parchment—or The Parchments plural, as it were."

"Yup. I had no idea...about any of it. First, I had no idea that there were so many and second I had no idea what was contained on them...you know, the information about all the believers."

"Anything else?" asked Michael.

"Actually, yeah…at first I thought that it was just a bunch of information on each believer cobbled together and set out in various columns with no connection. But, the information really tells a story. When you look at The Parchment on a particular day, it's like a snapshot in time of that person because each day The Parchment is updated…however, when you look at the different columns together and see where a particular person started out and compare it to where they end up….well, it tells you how that person is going to live their life."

"Yes…go on."

"Well, the Parchment tells the reader if the person is going to end up in the same classification as where they began. It tells you if they improve or regress. It tells you if they've reached their life destiny. It tells you the rank of their Guardian Angel. If a person Below listed in the Parchment is an Exister but is to finish off as Content and has not yet accomplished their life destiny, then the reader knows—pretty much—that this person is going to change somewhat and start living their life somewhat differently in order to join the ranks of the Content—and at some point accomplish their destiny. One example could be that wife I observed during my first Period that I told you about. Maybe she will break out of just existing and follow her dreams."

"How does The Parchment know of this change or non-change that is to take place in the future?" asked Michael still pressing Doc for answers.

"Because it's *God's* Parchment and He knows exactly where everyone is going to end up. He does the updating too, you know."

"Well, yes, I did know, but how did you know?"

"Woody told me," Doc said with a smile. "I don't think God physically opens all the books and manually updates each page with a new date or each person's information as to whether they've accomplished their destiny. He just does it. I don't know how. That's just the way it is. Maybe it's the same way He makes the sun always rise in the east day after day. It just happens. And the same for the updates—day after day—it just happens. He sees to it."

"I see…that's a good enough explanation for me because quite frankly, that's about how I figure He does it too. Maybe a touch hard to grasp…but what isn't hard to grasp about God? …a very lovable yet mysterious man He is. No one Below nor any of us up Here will ever understand His ways thoroughly."

"So did The Parchment confirm anything for you?" added Michael.

"Yeah, it confirmed that it is entirely within one's freedom Below to accomplish any destiny they want: a retail store manager, a musician, a cobbler, an aircraft pilot or a really good parent. Destinies, like success, come in all shapes and sizes. And, as hard as it is to admit this, now I agree with you totally that it might very well be someone's destiny to live in unhappiness and debt. That is a very plausible destiny for so many people. Another plausible destiny for many people will be to live their entire life blaming others. It's their destiny because they made it so. If they change, then obviously it won't be their destiny. God gave everybody Below the free will to live their life as they choose. That's why The Parchment notes that some people will stay in their same classification throughout their life while it also notes that some people will decide to change at some point. They'll change their destiny from what might have been a Blamer to one of the Content."

"Anything else?"

"Yes, I suppose it also tells a little about how their life Below will be lived depending on what rank of Guardian Angel they've been given. If someone in their adult life still has a Basic Guardian Angel, then chances are that person—as predicted by God—won't be in need of much teaching or guiding. They'll just be living. Whereas if The Parchment shows that a Junior has been assigned then it's clear that the person *might* be open to change where rudimentary guiding and teaching from Above might come in handy. Of course, if a Senior is assigned, then God knows that this person is on the move—whether it's within the same classification or crossing into other classifications—and that this person Below is ready to accept all the guiding, teaching and signs that their Senior can provide. Those two, I think, will be on an exceptional journey with a great destination as their result. Even though, perhaps, neither the One Below nor the Guardian Angel know what that destination might be. Am I right?" asked Doc, finishing off his summation.

"To a 'T' my boy...good for you," congratulated Michael.

"Although, I'm still unclear as to why there is a column in The Parchment that says 'Destiny Accomplished' yet it doesn't reveal what that destiny is. It doesn't say that this person is going to be a heart surgeon or a beachcomber or a farmer or the owner of a shoe store. The column just has a check mark or no check mark. It leaves out what the actual accomplishment is. How come?" asked Doc.

"Well, because if you know what your assignment's destiny is then you won't be able to guide and teach in an objective manner. Your ability to communicate in an unbiased manner will be fettered by your knowledge of that person's destiny. You'll steer them too hard in one direction. Trust me, it's better if you don't know what that person's destiny might be."

Doc nodded.

"Your job," Michael continued, "is to help your One Below understand life through signs and unspoken communication and hopefully help them make proper decisions. Your job is not to steer. They will steer the direction of their life as they choose. Where they steer is up to them. It is they who have to reach their destina-tion—whatever that destination might be—by their own free will. If you know what their destiny is then you would try too hard to steer them in one direction or another. That would just mess things up...no, really. Help them understand life and help them towards gaining happiness by guiding them and you'll take them a few steps closer to their destiny."

Doc listened in silence.

"Someone's destiny and destination is only knowable by God. He knows where they will end up...and only Him. While on the journey of life not even the One Below will understand fully where it is they are going—nor will their Guardian Angel. It's not your job to know. It's your job to guide and help along that path when needed. Got it?" asked the Archangel.

"Yeah, that makes sense, I suppose. Because even when I lived Below I recall not really knowing where my life would take me, rather I kept trying to point myself in a relatively positive direction knowing that things would always work out in the end. Now I know that—at least for people who are willing to let life lead them—the concepts of things working out in the end and Guardian Angels' work are closely intertwined. In fact, they might even be viewed as synonymous at times."

"You're learning again, my boy," Michael said with a smile.

"Oh, one more thing about The Parchment that I didn't quite understand. Why doesn't God list the date of death in the Parchment for people who haven't died yet? He knows when they are going to die, doesn't He?" asked Doc.

"Yes, He knows. Doc," the Archangel said kindly and quietly as he continued his explanation. "You will be working very closely with your new assignment Below. Closer than you were to your assignments you had when you were a Basic and Junior. Although the two of you will never formally meet both of you will become very attached to the other. How would you like it if you knew when one of your friends was going to die? You can't do your work properly if you know when your One Below is going to die. You have to do the best you can in the time you're given; so do they. Both of you know that death can come at any time, so it's best just to live life as best you can, while you can. Knowing when your assignment is going to die would prove too heavy a burden for you to carry. Besides, knowing that information would compromise your ability to guide and teach. Both of you must live life not knowing the unknowable. Only God knows—it's best that way."

"Yeah, that would be hard knowing when someone close to you was going to die. And I can see your point about not being able to do our work objectively if we knew beforehand when they were going to die. I guess we'd try to force things, eh? ...instead of allowing them to steer their own course."

"See, you're getting everything just fine. Everything is falling into place, isn't it?"

Doc nodded in agreement.

"Now, about these award shows you observed. Too much spare time on your hands...is that why you took in all these banquets?"

"No, not at all," replied Doc, "I wanted to see what people were doing for entertainment besides being addicted to reality T.V. and the consumption of stuff. It was just a fluke that all those award shows happened to be on in that one week. By the way, they were very instructive you know."

"Riiiiight. Hmmph, is that so...you learned something from these shows did you? Please, do tell. Enlighten me with thy wisdom, O powerful one," Michael added wryly.

"Well, I learned that a great number of very successful people in all walks of life thanked the same person in their acceptance speeches—and I don't mean mothers or fathers either."

"Oh, let me guess," started Michael sarcastically, "they thanked their producers and managers? That's the politically correct thing to do you know...thank the hand that feeds."

"No, no. I mean different people thanked the *same* person, not different people with the same job description. There's one person who has consistently been mentioned more often than others year in and year out in all the awards shows. I know, I did a little research."

"Like who?"

"God."

"*God?*" asked Michael. "What does He have to do with these awards shows?"

"Lots of things," Doc said, as he started his explanation. "At least that's what many of the winners said. Many of them thought God had a lot to do with their success in their chosen field, and said as much in their speeches. Many thanked God for making all things possible...including their success."

"Well, it is true, that anything is possible through God. Romans 8:28, I think... No wait, John 15:7. Well, it was one of them," said Michael, with a sheepish look on his face, barely covering his embarrassment of not knowing quite exactly the Bible quote he was looking for. "Oh look, a pretty dove. My, they're wonderful birds."

Doc looked skyward. "I don't see a dove."

"No? Hmm, it must have quickly flown behind that tree. Quick too, aren't they."

"Yes, I guess so..."

"Must have..." Michael started fidgeting with the seeds in his pocket and nervously gazed out over the grass looking for Edmund. "Now where *did* that chipmunk get to? I have another handful of food for him."

"Michael, don't forget the inscription on the front of The New Academy. And, Luke says it too at 18:27...just for future reference."

"Edmund....heeeere, Edmund."

"Aaaaaanyway, then after the speeches," continued Doc, "I thought about what I had heard and sort of compared it to a team effort—the team being three people: God, the person Below and the Guardian Angel. God is the captain of the team and will lead the team to great success if given a chance. The person Below is the worker and main beneficiary of the team and if the person truly buys into the team concept then great things await them. Of course, we Guardian Angels fit into this team insofar that we can act as guides for the person Below if they ever need a little help in manoevering around life's challenges while they are enroute to their destination."

"Sooooo, Michael, *that's* what I took away from all those award shows. And, don't think God doesn't smile when His name is mentioned during the Academy or Grammy Awards. Or the small town awards shows. I think He likes the attention," said Doc as he finished off his explanation with a grin. "Oh, one more thing, when a person Below publicly recognizes God in a high-profile event, the Galleries go crazy. There's hooting and hollering; screaming and cheering. It's a really happy time."

"Wow," exclaimed Michael, "even I never noticed that connection before. Good for you. Usually, the only thing I got out of the all the glitz of the entertainment awards were what the pictures in *BEN* showed…you know…what not to wear out in public. For all the talent and ability that many of those people possess, some seem to lose their head when it comes to wardrobe issues on the big night. No, really though, some of those outfits should never rightly see the light of day. Have you ever seen the likes of them?"

"Suuuure," replied Doc, who thought to himself that it was hardly Michael's place to be commenting on fashion. Michael was known for not being up on the latest styles.

"And one more thing," started Doc. "I also took in a sold-out concert of the baddest boys of rock, Motley Crue, one night in Gallery 97. It was great. But one of the best things about the concert was when Vince Neil, the lead singer, was leaving the stage at the end of the show, he turned around and shouted in the microphone to 15,000 screaming fans……'God Bless.' Michael, you should have heard the Gallery. Every Guardian Angel went wild….just like the fans down Below at the show. Now, probably not everyone at the concert heard it, but I bet some kids did. Who knows, maybe those two words were heard by someone who wants to believe and that just might have been the two words they needed to hear to start them on their road to believing. Even bad boys of rock believe."

"Of course, they do. Well, some of them anyway. You don't think they get where they are all on their own do you?"

Wanting to get back to more of what Doc had learned, the Archangel was just about to ask Doc about what he knew about Seekers. Sensing the question and not quite being ready yet to answer, Doc made his move.

"Michael, do you mind if I take my leave a little early. I have to…"

"Leave?" asked Michael. "Leave…why? Where are you going?"

"I'd like to look at my notes once more before I head out for my fourth Observational Period, if you don't mind. You can never review too much you know."

"Sure, you go. I have to head over to Scotty and Slash's Record Shop anyway…I hear they *just* got their hands on a bootleg copy of a song released Below a few years back by Pearl Jam—'Life Wasted.' Supposed to be quite good. Aaaaanyway, see you in ten days—same ti…"

"No time for entertainment, eh?"

"Never you mind. Besides, Pearl Jam isn't just entertainment, they're perfection, dude. Oh, make no mistake, God created music; Pearl Jam just perfected it. It's a fact. Look it up."

Doc smiled. "Ok, same time, same place."

With that, both Angels went their separate ways—Michael seeking more music and Doc seeking more answers.

23

SIGNS

There were still two things that Doc had yet to understand fully: the qualities of a Seeker and the art of unspoken communication—that is, the sending of signs in an attempt to guide and teach. He was slowly piecing both concepts together, but there was still more to learn.

Doc had engaged a little in sending signs to his previous assignments Below when he was a Junior, but not to the extent he would need to undertake as a Senior. He knew that the key to being a great Senior was predicated on being an expert in the craft of unspoken communication. Doc also knew that the success of his assignment Below would also be dependent upon how his assignment listened to his instruction, viewed those signs, interpreted them and then acted on them. And how the One Below did those things was in turn based on how the Guardian Angel sent forth those signs. The success of the One Below depended on the Guardian Angel Above, and the success of the Guardian Angel Above depended on the One Below.

The Academy saw that Doc had engaged a little in the craft and it was this reason why the Academy decided to move him up when they did. Doc seemed to have a knack for sending subtle hints to his assignments Below right at the opportune moment. He did this in the hopes that they might pick up on the signs, thus helping them with a decision they had to make or to guide them to which path to take at a certain moment.

But the sending of signs and the art of unspoken communication wasn't used that often by Doc during previous assignments. True, he used signs more than other Basic and Junior Guardian Angels, but, the fact of the matter was, Doc still had a lot to learn about the great craft of unspoken communication. Most of the unspoken communication Doc engaged in while he was a Basic and Junior had to do with safety issues, like sending subtle signs to get the One Below to slow down in their car—not so much about guiding. It was nothing so big as trying to get his assignment to ask a certain person to marry them or to get them to change their career. Work of a Senior was big business.

More often than not, it was a learning process that took a great deal of time to master for both the One Below and the Guardian Angel Above. The Guardian Angel had to know when to send signs, what kind of signs to send and what events those signs would manifest into down Below.

The Guardian Angel would send a sign—a very deliberate sign. However, people Below would sometimes just see the sign as a regular event or happening in their everyday life. There was no piece of paper attached to the event saying, 'The person you just met in the airport will change your life—pay attention to them.' No, the One Below had to perceive the event or happening as a sign and not just something that happened to them. The key to getting an assignment to act on a sign was in fact getting the One Below to perceive it as just that—a sign. They had to see the event as happening for a reason. Getting One Below to distinguish between a sign and just a plain old everyday occurrence was the tough part. It was all about trial and error.

After the One Below perceived the otherwise non-event as a sign that had a meaning to it, then the One Below would have to interpret the sign in order to actually find out what meaning lay beyond the event. After deciphering the meaning, the One Below would have to act upon it—hopefully—properly.

Depending on the Guardian Angel and the assignment—their characteristics, where they were leading their life and the like—signs, under the guise of inconsequential events, might come often or few and far between. Regardless of the frequency, the success rate of having each sign perceived as such, interpreted correctly and acted upon properly, was not high. However, over time, as the Guardian Angel became better at sending signs and better at the art of unspoken communication, and the One Below learned a little more about life, paid more attention to the smallest of events, became a better listener and then learned how to capitalize on those events, the success rate improved.

In each chain of events there was great room for error. But when an event was perceived as a sign and thus culminated in the One Below acting on it correctly, it brought happiness Above and the One Below one step closer to their destination—and thus one step closer to realizing their goals and dreams, and possibly their destiny.

The journey of realizing one's destiny and dreams Below took time—years or, in some cases, decades. It also took patience while waiting for that success to materialize. Of course, in the meantime, it took hard work on behalf of the One Below to continually move towards their goals and happiness. Happiness and success, in many cases and in any form, can take years to materialize.

Most people Below seemed to feel that they did not have the time to wait nor the energy to expend towards making their dreams and goals come true. More often than not, they would settle for whatever lot in life happened to come their way.

Many just existed: they could not see the future for the present. Others blamed: they could not see the future for the past. But some, were on the lookout for more. And those—those who were on the lookout for more—well, they usually started their quest by listening to their souls. For where your soul is, there will your destiny be also.

24

oLeh, e.v., johnny d. and wa'Lah

Doc started his fourth Observational Period at one of the Galleries in the hopes of picking up some tips on what the qualities of Seekers were and what the key to unspoken communication was.

While there, Doc saw many of his old friends and met new Guardian Angels that he had never met before. Some were Juniors, others Seniors. They had carriage over people Below in all the classifications: Existers, Blamers, Content and some Seekers.

Doc noticed that there were some Guardian Angels leaning intently over the railing watching their Ones Below. Others were off in the corner playing cards and still others were engaged in light conversation and seemed otherwise unoccupied.

Doc saw a couple of his old friends in the corner playing cards.

He knew them when he was a Junior and they had been promoted to Seniors about a year before Doc.

"Well hello, E.V., my old friend," started Doc, "is the Guardian business so slow that you have to while away your time with hazardous games of chance and cards? Does Michael know you guys are playing? And Oleh, not you too? How *are* you guys?" Doc asked with a grin.

E.V. was deep in thought, wondering if his three 9 of hearts would be enough to best Oleh's hand. "Doc, I am rolling," said Oleh not worrying about E.V.'s wondering. "How you doing…haven't seen you for a bit?"

"I'm great, thanks…just thought I would come over to the Gallery today and see what was going on here. Had I known you had a game going on I would've brought my money pouch. Well, on second thought, maybe I wouldn't have—I'm in my fourth Observational Period so I should be observing. So, tell me, is the Guardian business so slow that cards now occupy most of your time?"

"Ha! No, not really, but my old assignment—a Content—just died and there was some type of administrative mix-up regarding my next assignment. I was slated for a Seeker, but instead I was given an Exister…not for too long, though; they say that I should have my real assignment within a weeks time. Bureaucracy…some things never change," said Oleh, as he threw in a denarius, upping E.V.'s bet.

"And that's the reason why you find yourself in the middle of a high stakes card game?" asked Doc.

"Sort of. The fact is, there's nothing to do when you have an Exister. Especially when they're not on the move, as it were. Or at least there's very little to do. All they do is exist. No guiding or teaching to do. Just the odd bit of protecting and guarding…you know, the stuff we learned in Basic. Very few signs need be put forth. They wouldn't be seen anyway even if I did give out a few. Quite boring, actually. Once in a while I check in just to see if they're doing alright, but there's really nothing much to do day in and day out.

They just go through life accepting that their lot at present is what it will be like to the end of their days. Seems they're going nowhere fast. E.V. calls it 'life wasted,' don't you? Oh well, this little mix-up gives me a chance for a short break. To no great mischief, I suppose, other than the mischief I get into playing cards with these miscreants," Oleh said, as he waved his arm towards, E.V, Johnny D.—who always bet using pieces of eight and shillings—and Wa'Lah, the camel master, who wagered camels when his dirham ran out.

"No, to no great mischief, I suppose" agreed Doc. He never had been given an Exister and he really didn't want one. "Hey, anyone I know over at the railing?"

"Hmmm, I don't think so," answered E.V. in his unmistakeable baritone, finally looking up from his hand, "but go watch anyway…I think they're mostly Seniors so there's always new stuff to learn from them. Even Marco will tell you that although he's an Advanced, he learns something new every day… Yes, yes, I know it's my turn to play…easy Wa'Lah, don't get your turban in a knot… Sorry Doc, these guys get a little unruly if the game is held up…talk to you later, okay?"

"Sure, you keep playing…I'll be over at the railing," Doc said, just as he heard Johnny exclaim, "What do you say to three shillings?" Doc left the card game and headed over to the railing to see what he could learn from the Seniors that were guiding and sending signs right at that moment.

Doc stayed until nightfall. He met many Seniors and asked many questions about Seekers, patience, signs and the art of unspoken communication. His observing and questions lasted for hours. He received many of the answers he had been looking for. Some questions went unanswered. Finally, it was time to go home and get some sleep.

As he left, he looked over his shoulder into the back corner and saw that Oleh, E.V., Johnny D. and Wa'Lah hadn't moved an inch. As he walked home, he passed a young boy, Gamm, with a camel in tow heading for the gallery. It seemed Wa'Lah had had better nights.

The next day and the day after and the day after that he went to other Galleries and learned from the Guardian Angels who were practicing their craft there. He met as many Seniors as he could. He observed and listened. He asked questions and sought answers. Making mental notes of each encounter, Doc was slowly seeing how top-end guarding fit in with life Below.

Doc neared the end of his fourth Observational Period the same way he started it—going to the Galleries and experiencing other Seniors at work first hand: how they interacted with their assignment Below and how their assignment Below picked up their signs. For Doc, it was all coming together—finally. He was pleased with the knowledge he had gained, and slowly he was becoming confident in his ability to join the full rank of Senior, ready to take carriage of a Seeker. Michael never told Doc for sure that he would be getting a Seeker, but it was possible he would be given one. If so, he had to be ready, even though he still didn't know what set Seekers apart. Even with all his observing, Doc hadn't come across that many Seekers. Seekers were hard to come by.

Doc had one more day to make sense of it all before he met Michael for his fourth Interview. He had decided that he had done enough observing and he needed some time to think about all he had learned and to piece it all together. He decided to spend this last day at his lake. If he had any puzzling questions she would silently help him find the answers. She always did.

25

pure joy! seekers!

Bright and early Doc was down by her shores tending to his favourite spot along her water's edge. At first, Doc worked in silence. When they weren't talking about life, using words and ripples, both liked to converse in silence. Doc could be by her shores cleaning or just enjoying the sun and breeze on her sandy beach for hours without saying a word, yet he always felt that he had just finished having the most intense conversation with her. Doc figured she felt the same way too.

Finally Doc spoke to his lake. "I'm getting it, you know," he started. "I'm finally seeing how all this stuff fits together. I never really understood destinies and goals when I was Below because I just lived my own life and never really paid attention to what else was going on around me. I never thought about people just existing or whatever. I went to school, worked, believed in God and was happy. When I lived Below I always knew I had a Guardian Angel but back then, you never wonder about what it's like on their side. But now, I think I'm finally understanding some things that I never realized before. I think I'm finally understanding how it all works."

The lake didn't respond. But the slight ripples on her surface beckoned a further explanation. After all, it had been some time since Doc had visited her. She was more than ready to have her friend sit down and chat with her once again.

Doc sat down on his favourite rock and started telling his lake about some of the things he learned during all his Observational Periods.

"First," said Doc to his friend, "people Below are the master of their own destinies. They can live their life Below any way they see fit. They can spend it in jail or they can govern a country. It matters not. Both avenues are open, with few exceptions, to everybody. It is open to them to just exist their way through life and it is also open to them to blame others if their lot in life is not what they had hoped for."

The lake was silent, but she seemed to be soaking up all of what Doc was telling her.

"It is also open for people to be content and happy with their lives—happy with the life they've created for themselves and their family. They don't see the need to blame others or change anything. They have worked hard for their happiness and are content with the fruits of their labour."

"Happiness," continued Doc, "is hard work, you know. Far harder work than what is needed to be unhappy. Unhappiness just takes self-reinforcement that you're unhappy. Happiness must be worked for. And, to attain it, it sometimes takes patience. Happiness is open to all people. You don't have to be educated to be happy."

"And make no mistake, happiness can come in different forms. There is the material form, where someone is happy because they have a good job, a good family and may have a little surplus money to buy a few extra items now and again. And then, there is the spiritual form of happiness whereby, regardless of their lot in life, they are happy from the inside out because of their deep belief in God. They experience the happiness that He brings to each person when He is invited into their lives as a friend."

"Most people think that God is all-powerful all the time. That's kind of true, if you get my meaning," Doc explained to his lake. "However, He's really only as powerful as the person Below allows Him to be. So, if you take the other side of the coin, God can be completely powerless also. The power of God is entirely up to the person Below. Imagine, the power of God being controlled by the One Below."

"You see, it's like this, my friend," said Doc as he dipped his toes into her warm waters, "if someone Below buys into the power of God and all that He stands for then really good things can be accomplished. There becomes a team of three: God, the One Below and us. We're there to send signs now and then to the person Below to help them stay on the right path—whatever that path may be. Only God knows. When the person Below picks up on the signs it's *as if* some strange force or coincidence is conspiring in their favour. But really, it's God's will that's being done and we're just the messengers seeing that it gets done."

Doc carried on his oration to his glistening friend.

"To see God's will done takes patience, just like true happiness takes patience. Part of my job is to instill a sense of patience in my assignment through signs and unspoken communication. Just like you and I in a way. You don't answer me, but you always talk to me and speak to me and see me through my problems. In a way, Guardian Angels perform the same function. Our assignments Below can't see us and we can't speak to them, but we're always there and sending signs when needed. And we're always talking to them through unspoken communication. They just have to feel it and believe it insofar that they know something great will be waiting at the end of their journey—their destiny. What that destiny will be no one knows. But if it's God's will, what it is or how big it is, it matters not. Regardless of the end result it will be pure joy."

In a flash, Doc beamed with excitement.

"That's it, my friend! That's it!" Doc exclaimed to the lake just realizing that his conversation with the lake had helped him uncover the mystery of what a Seeker was and what Michael kept meaning when he referred to Pure Joy.

"Pure Joy! Seekers!"

"Seekers! Pure Joy! That's the defining quality of a Seeker."

"That's what Michael was referring to awhile back. He always said that when a person Below *really* bought into the team and the power of God, Pure Joy would result. He also said that when an assignment Below was 'in sync' with his Guardian Angel, picking up on signs and acting accordingly, then Pure Joy would surely follow. Pure Joy! Of course! How could I not see it before?"

Doc kicked his feet in the water and watched the splashes descend back down to the surface. The new ripples in the water gave the surface life. He smiled at his friend and her ripples smiled back.

"God's will done is the Pure Joy…and only *Seekers* understand that their purpose on Earth is to see God's will done. God's will for a Seeker could be as a janitor, a good parent, a priest or pastor or as a philanthropic billionaire. It doesn't matter! What matters is that the Seeker strives to see the will of God done. Seeing the will of God done will be Pure Joy. Seekers are strivers!"

"Everybody on the team will feel it. God smiles because He knows that the person Below is following their true destiny—a destiny he always hoped for…His true destiny for them. The person Below smiles for having reached their dreams after a long hard journey, and we Guardian Angels smile because we know we had a hand in helping our assignment Below on the long path to their destination. Michael will be so pleased that I've figured out what he meant by Pure Joy. Thank you, thank you my friend, for talking with me," said Doc gratefully to his lake as left for home.

That night, remembering the conversation with his lake, Doc fell asleep with a smile on his face while reading the Bible—just in case the Archangel had any Scripture quizzes for him...even though it was Michael who needed a little brushing up.

26

WISDOM

The next day, Doc arrived early at their bench. He really didn't want to go through the routine of trying to explain to the Archangel that he wasn't really late, but was rather right on time. Doc shut his eyes and in his mind put together the pieces of the puzzle he had been working on the last few weeks. Some pieces were the concepts he learned in Senior Theory. Other pieces were how he could help his One Below. And still others were just about life in general.

But, to Doc, they all had either a bit—or a lot—to do with God.

That's going to be hard, Doc said to himself, getting people Below to buy into the strength of the team and the limitless power of God. I know that many people believe in God, but most have yet to unleash His true power—His true lovingkindness. All I can hope for is that I am successful in guiding my assignment Below towards believing in God and joining the team. Too bad more people Below weren't team players.

Doc also thought that it was too bad more people didn't treat God like a new product they're purchasing for the first time.

Give God, like a new product, a trial run, thought Doc. New products come with a money-back guarantee and a trial period. If the person doesn't like the product then they can just return it if they don't like it, thought Doc, as he remembered one of the gimmicks companies used Below when courting the purchaser into buying their wares.

Only my product—God—thought Doc to himself, comes with an even better guarantee. He comes with a trial period too, only it's better: there's no money needed up front! And, the trial period could last as long or as little as the consumer wanted. Now that's putting the customer first.

Anyone could take advantage of my free trial period: people Below who didn't believe at all and wanted to become fair-weather-believers-in-times-of-crisis who thought that God might be able to help them during their times of crisis; or, fair-weather-believers-in-times-of-crisis who wanted to become more permanent believers—people who wanted to let God take more control over their life, especially if they were having a hard time managing it on their own. Yes sir, I'm a Heavenly salesman, my free trial period is open to absolutely everyone—no discriminatory selling practices up Here. None at all.

"Step right up, get your free God trial period. No money down. No money needed," Doc sang with a chuckle.

Doc figured potential buyers Below could try Him out for, say, six months or a year, by allowing God to lead their life. All they had to do was point themselves in a relatively positive direction and let God, the Guardian Angel assigned and life, do the rest. That's another good thing about the trial offer—it would lower the Guardian Angel unemployment lines Above as every trial consumer would automatically receive a Guardian Angel if they didn't have one assigned already. I'll bet the unemployment office would be happy with that.

When trying God out, and if they really give Him and us a chance to do our work, then I'll bet they will find their lot in life will improve tenfold. Their happiness will return, I'm sure of it. Of course, it will take time, because happiness takes hard work. But instead of trying to find happiness with just themselves looking, people Below will now have three people on the search team.

If they're not satisfied they can always reject Him and turn away from God and the team. After all, they are completely free to go back to being a Blamer at anytime they want. And the beauty of it is that it hasn't cost them a cent. That might be a good thing for the people Below who don't have two cents to rub together.

"There," said Doc to the open air around the bench, "there's my sales pitch for the all new 'Unleash the Power of God' free trial period."

Silently, Doc hoped that there would be a sudden decrease in unemployed Guardian Angels—but he wasn't holding his breath.

He looked around to see if Michael was in sight, but he couldn't see the Archangel anywhere. "Oh well," Doc said aloud, "he is the Archangel and I suppose he arrives exactly when he's supposed to."

Still waiting, Doc did more reflecting. He was genuinely pleased with what he had learned over the last little bit. It was true, he had gained more knowledge. Even when he was over at the Gallery during his last Observational Period, another Guardian Angel remarked on his wisdom. A young Basic Guardian Angel had come up to Doc and said she hoped to gain as much wisdom as Doc had.

After that encounter, Doc went home and thought about that. He wasn't convinced he was wiser than any other—in fact, he knew he wasn't. But meeting the young Angel made him think about the difference between knowledge and wisdom. And while sitting on the bench waiting for Michael, Doc made the distinction.

Knowledge, comes from school, reading what others have written, talking with peers. You need knowledge to become a brain surgeon or an astronaut. But you don't need knowledge to be happy. You need *wisdom* to be happy.

And I know, Doc thought to himself, wisdom comes from within. People don't need knowledge to be happy—they need wisdom. The wisdom needed—and it's not a lot—to truly live and strive is within you. The wisdom, that is, the mental component, needed for people to change their lives for the better or make their life a happy one is already inside their bodies…inside their soul. People are looking to knowledge and education to make them happy; but it doesn't take education to be happy, it takes wisdom. Knowledge is learned from the outside. Wisdom comes from within, not without. Everybody is born with wisdom—it's just that you have to look for it and uncover it.

Doc knew he was on the right track.

Doc laughed a disbelieving laugh. I guess that's why so many people are unhappy or are searching for things they will never find. They're looking in the wrong place. Most people think that happiness and destinies and dreams are found on the outside. True, accomplishment does, in many cases, come in the form of reaching a pinnacle at work or wherever, but other than that, satisfaction comes from within. That's why people are having a hard time finding it. Because *within* is the last place they look—if ever.

They're looking to material things to make them happy. All they need to do is uncover the wisdom that is already in their soul and happiness will be just under it. Wisdom, happiness, resiliency of the human body and mind—it all comes from within. From within the soul. The soul is the keeper of wisdom. Wisdom is the keeper of happiness. Too bad more people don't open the door to their soul. They'd be surprised at what they'd find.

Doc kept his mind working. That's why the simplest problems go unsolved. The simplest problems in life can't be solved with knowledge; they need wisdom to be solved and everybody has wisdom in their soul. Everybody. All they need to do is look and listen in the right place to find it. It's there. Wisdom isn't the only thing within our souls. So is God. Maybe more people should listen to their souls. They might be surprised at what they'll hear.

27

cakes, chess...and mad scientists

Finally, Doc spotted the Archangel walking towards their bench. With Edmund in hand, Michael was singing some song by Kid Rock. Or, perhaps Pearl Jam.

No, wait, Doc thought, that sounds like a song from Bon Jovi or STP. No...no. Huh...it sounds like maybe Disturbed or is it The Edge playing Until the End of the World. Whatever it is, it is starting to sound more like somebody shouting at the devil than a song. Who it was, Doc could not tell, mainly because the Archangel, even though he thought himself a rock star, was anything but.

Good thing Michael doesn't quit his day job, Doc mused, because his singing isn't the greatest...ah, I know...it's The Cult.

"Doc, my boy," the Archangel said with a big smile, "how are you doing this fine day?"

"Michael, I am rolling," answered Doc. "And, what brings you in such high spirits?"

"Oh, nothing in particular, just happy to be alive, I suppose. But I was away for a few days, so it is good to be back home. Ah, home sweet home," replied Michael.

"But anyway, why am I happy? A wise man once told me that 'happiness comes from within, not without.' And I dare say that my innards are happy today," Michael said with a knowing grin. "Ever think about that little bit of philosophy?"

Doc smiled in return but said nothing for a moment. A wise man? Who is wiser than the Archangel? Ahhh, it must be God he's referring to. God must have told him that happiness comes from within. Doc's smile beamed even brighter as he reassured himself that he was on the right track with his wisdom dilemma and the like.

"So, what shall we talk about today, O wise one," asked Doc.

"Wise? You think I'm wise, do you? Well, I thank you for the vote of confidence, but let me make this clear and I'll only tell you once...wisdom, like happiness, my lad, comes from within, not without. Everybody has wisdom in their soul...they just have to listen for it. Everybody Below is born with wisdom—but few ever unlock it. Clear?" asked Michael.

Doc smiled again. "Crystal."

"Now, back to your question...what was it?...oh yes, what are we going to talk about today? How about you tell me? How about you tell me what you observed during your last Period," said the Archangel as he put more seeds in his hand to please Edmund's seemingly never-ending appetite.

"Well," started Doc, "I spent quite a bit of time at Gallery 97 although I did go to others too." Gallery 97 was Doc's favourite Gallery; Gallery 93D was another one of his favourites along with 129E. All were close to home, so he could easily walk there in just a few minutes. All Galleries were good spots to learn and hang out with other Guardian Angels, but it just seemed to Doc that the fellowship and camaraderie at these three Galleries were better than others.

"I know this Gallery 97 that you speak of," said Michael, as if he was remembering fondly some of his younger guarding days. "But it seems to me," Michael added with a raised eyebrow, "that there is more fun being had at that Gallery than learning and guarding. Am I right?"

"Well, yes, there might be more card games going on in that Gallery than others, and sometimes they feed stray camels, but I still find that I can learn a lot there. Many Seniors and Advanced go there, you know. They seem to be able to find the right mix of work and pleasure. Anyway, I spent much of my last Period there."

"Very well, and what did you observe…besides the card games that is?"

"I saw many Seniors at work, day in and day out. I observed who they were guarding and guiding. I saw them practicing the art of unspoken communication by sending signs. I saw many assignments Below pick up on those signs and many that didn't. I saw Seniors sending certain signs to their assignments Below in the hopes that they would exercise patience in this situation or that. The situations where their Guardian Angels were sending signs to be patient were varied. Some of the situations involved personal relationships, some involved the signing of legal contracts and some involved things such as purchasing things they couldn't really afford. Delay, as you know is the best remedy for anger. And I think delay and patience is the best remedy to stay out of debt. I think we spoke about this concept awhile back. That is, if people were a little more patient in all facets of their life then things in the end might work out a little better. You know, instead of rushing into things."

"Hmmm, yes, we did discuss that if I recall correctly," said Michael. "Soooo, tell me, how does one go about practicing the art of un-spoken communication? How is Doc going to send these signs to his new assignment Below?"

"Well, since you asked, I think it goes something like this," said

Doc knowing that this question was one of the two big questions the Archangel would ask—the other being what a Seeker is.

"For starters," Doc said, as he watched Edmund climb out of the Archangel's hand and run off to his hole with a mouthful of seeds exploding at the lips, "my assignment believes in God, I know that... now. So, at least partially they will be open to the fact that God and Guardian Angels are hard at work for them. To what extent they believe in God, or to what extent they believe that their Guardian Angel will be helping them, remains to be seen. It's up to them, I suppose. I guess I'll figure out the depth of their belief when I get to know who they really are. Who they are on the inside, that is."

"Good...go on."

"And I now know that my job is not only to protect their physical well-being—the thing we're usually known for—but also, part of the job is to guide them in their everyday life. Open their mind to the possibilities for the future. Get them to notice opportunities and make good use of them. Get them to act on hunches...acting on a hunch might very well be the first step towards unlocking a soul and finding a destiny. Of course, I don't know what the future holds for them and neither do they but as long as they point themselves in a relatively positive direction I'll do my best to present opportunities that will take them one step closer to their destination...whatever that may be."

"Uh huh...I see...what else."

"Well, at times, the road to their destiny might be a hard road to follow...there will be obstacles...because happiness and success are themselves hard roads to follow. If they are at risk of going off course or if the burden is more than they can bear, then I'll nudge them back on course and help them with the burden. After all, God has said that He will allow no person to suffer a temptation that is more than they can handle and with that temptation He will also provide the means of escape. I'll be there to ease their temptation, say, maybe the temptation to give up their journey. Along with seeing them through the temptation, I'll also provide them with an opportunity to escape it, thereby hopefully keeping them on their path to happiness and success. Of course, a lot of my success depends on them…it depends on the strength of their belief."

"And patience," asked Michael, "how does patience fit into all of this?"

"Patience comes in, or should be used that is, in all components of their life. For instance, if they're getting impatient about maybe not seeing the fruits of their labour then I'll try and suggest they be patient for awhile. Destinies don't happen overnight, Michael. They take to time to form. Destiny is like a baked good…like a cake. There are many ingredients. Before you have a finished cake you need all the ingredients. You also have to have all the ingredients present at the same time. When making a cake, with all the ingredients at hand you can then mix them together and bake them. At the end of the baking time, you have your finished cake. Destinies need baking too…they need time to come together. For destinies—the baking, that is—the time needed to realize the finished product is life. Once someone has all the ingredients that will bring them to their destiny, they have to keep living life until the finished product arrives. It's no good to cut the baking time short. Patience is needed to see you through till the end."

"A cake? You're comparing living life to a cake? Is that what you're saying?"

"Yes…a cake. Bakers have patience. So must Ones Below who are seeking their destiny."

"And that's only one example when patience will come in handy—when Ones Below are striving after their destiny. But patience can be used in all facets of their lives," added Doc.

"Like what?"

"Well, like buying things. We spoke of this earlier. People Below need to exercise patience in their spending habits. Not encumbered by debt, they will be better able to take that road to their destination if they're so inclined. But again, it's entirely up to them. After all, God gave them the free will to do anything they want. They can spend fifty years in jail if they want...or, they can take the road to their destiny. It's entirely up to them. If they choose the road to their destiny...God and Guardian Angels will see it done."

"How do you know?"

"It just is."

"Well, that's a great philosophy to live by, Doc, but what signs are you going to use to help your assignment on the journey?"

"What signs am I going to use? ...Is that what you asked me?"

"Yes, what signs."

"What...do you want me to list for you all the signs I'm going to use in every situation for every problem my assignment Below encounters? If I remember correctly that would be like someone asking the reason why everything happens and if I further remember correctly, that question is unanswerable," said Doc with a smile, remembering that the Archangel gave him a hard time when he asked Michael why everything happens.

"Ok, fine, just one will do...tell me one sign that you might employ when guiding your assignment Below."

"Well, I'll present opportunities...yes, opportunities. Don't forget Michael, part of my success is beholden to the ability of my assignment to know that things *do* happen for a reason. Many things in life just don't happen willy nilly you know. Some coincidences are no coincidences at all. There's powerful forces hard at work prodding Ones Below...suggesting, nudging."

Doc continued his explanation. "With that mindset—knowing that everything happens for a reason—then when I do in fact send signs or opportunities my assignment's way then they must perceive them as such. Then they interpret them. Then, act on them accordingly. They have the hard part...my part's easy..."

"Ah, yes," interjected Michael, "but if your signs are too weak or too strong then they won't be perceived as such. They'll just be viewed as an everyday occurrence with no meaning to them. So, viewed another way, the key is in the *quality* of the sign and not necessarily the mindset of the person Below. I would say that the key to having someone Below perceive a happening in their life as having meaning—or being a sign, if you will—depends on your ability to make your sign or opportunity distinguishable from a regular, earthly event. Then, your assignment Below, if he's attuned to the team effort, will have much greater success in perceiving it as a sign and will be then able to act accordingly. Make sense?" asked Michael.

For all Michael's aloofness and simplicity, Doc recognized that he was still the Archangel and still very knowledgeable about such things. "Yeah, that makes sense."

"And that's why, getting a person Below and their Guardian Angel on the same page takes time. Both have to feel the other out. The One Below needs time to become accustomed to how the team works and the Guardian Angel needs to know how the assignment Below reacts to certain suggestions or opportunities. Yes, it takes time, Doc. But, as you pointed out in one of your earlier Interviews, all people Below *have* is time. Time to change their destiny if they so please."

Doc nodded.

"Now, back to my question of earlier, how about you give me one example of a sign or of an opportunity you might employ during your journey with them to their destination—you know, the art of unspoken communication? Humour me, give me a 'for instance' on how you plan to use the art of unspoken communication when sending these signs you speak of," said Michael taking on the look and tone of official examiner instead of estranged rock star.

"Ok, for instance, if my assignment is at a stage in their life where they are looking for a change—for whatever reason—then I will send subtle signs confirming that change would be a good new path to follow."

"Maybe," Doc continued, "they want to change from being a debt-ridden Exister beholden to stuff to be one of the Content. They wouldn't know exactly what the urge is they're feeling nor what it meant. All they might feel is that something deep inside them has been awakened or a door deep inside has been opened and all they need are a few signs as to the meaning of it all. A few signs confirming that they should listen to this new, awakened feeling...even though at that moment they have no idea what it is."

Doc continued. "I might accompany them on last-minute shopping trips, ensuring that the latest fashion they really don't *need* but want is not available in their size. This initial setback might be just enough to start breaking the tyranny of their custom—the custom of spending money they don't have. Or, I might ensure the new couch they want but don't really *need* isn't available in a colour that will suit their living room. Those would be two signs telling them to listen closely to their awakened soul that wants to bust out of being in debt in order to forge a new path. Getting shut out a few times on needless shopping sprees might instill in them a sense of patience. If interpreted properly, the One Below might see them as signs. That is, signs letting them know that they didn't really need this stuff and other things—better things—await them around a corner."

"After a week or two they will realize that they didn't need that 'stuff' after all. After six months they will realize that they have money in their savings account instead of always being broke. This might then give them the incentive to pursue this course of patience or restraint for a while longer and after a year they might have enough money to take that trip they've always wanted to take to the country where their ancestors came from. I would make sure that when they were looking at airline prices, there would be seat sales to the country they wanted to visit."

"While there on their holiday, they might meet their true soulmate...the person God intended for them to marry. And that, that marriage, the marriage that made them happy, well, that might be their destiny. Their destiny in life might be to marry someone from a foreign land, become a great parent and be happy. All because they altered their spending habits a year or two before. And all because I made sure that a bunch of furniture was the wrong colour and the quiet whispering of their soul—yearning to burst out and change the custom of it's mind—should be listened to. And they listened! And, *voila!* Within a years time the tyranny of debt was over and the person was now married."

"You see Michael, everything is connected and everything happens for a reason. The reason might not be apparent right away, but even the simplest of events can turn into life-changing triumphs down the road if you give them time to play out…time to bake, if you get my meaning." Doc finished with a smile.

"Everything's connected is it?"

"Yes, everything is connected. The connection might not be easily spotted right away, but happenings in life are definitely connected. After all, I have a hand in bringing those happenings or things to pass. At least, the important things. The important things are connected. How can they not be? I'm hard at work making sure the connection is made. But to realize a life-changing connection takes time to materialize. Without patience, their spending habits will not be life-altering…they'll just be spending habits. However, if my assignment Below is open to the belief that things are connected and things will always work out if they let them, then at the other end, God and Guardian Angels are hard at work seeing that their patience and the belief in the team will result in them receiving their just rewards."

"Some might view that these things are happening for a reason because the earth is conspiring in their favour. I suppose that's true in a way. Oh, make no mistake, there's conspiring going on. But," said Doc with a mischievous grin on his face, "the conspiring is really being done by two people…God and a Guardian Angel. *We're the conspirators!*" He finished with an angelic, evilish laugh. "Muah… haha…ha."

Michael joined in. Soon both Angels were laughing uncontrollably like two mad scientists. After a moment or two they realized how silly they must have sounded. Looking around to see if anyone had seen their outburst and thus think them certifiably crazy, they descended back into reality.

"Muahhahaha..hahaha...haha..ha.....aha....ah....ahem...yes, well, so, you do believe, after all, that things happen for a reason, eh? Because I remember during one of our first conversations you weren't entirely sure on the matter," said Michael.

"I'm sure. And it's not just sending signs or engaging in unspoken communication that we undertake on behalf of our assignments. Our work also involves sending opportunities to Ones Below at the right moment...or chance meetings with someone. But if the meeting is orchestrated by us, then they're not chance at all, but rather planned meetings."

"In the same respect, for someone who is contemplating a job change, I might see to it that an opportunity arises which might just be the last confirmatory piece of the puzzle that the One Below needed to see before setting the course of their life on a new path."

"Take this, for example. Perhaps, there's somebody Below who goes to work Monday to Friday and never does anything with his time except watch T.V. But, for ten years, he has been struggling with a decision whether to leave his current job and apply for a completely new job or keep submitting to the tyranny of custom. Deciding that buying a lottery ticket would be the quick fix, the person Below buys his first newspaper in ten years to check to see if his ticket is a winner. It's not a winner, and as he throws the paper down in disappointment the paper lands open on the 'Careers' section—and staring him right in the face is an ad advertising *exactly* the job he had contemplated applying for asking for *exactly* the qualifications he possessed."

"The decision to buy the lottery ticket, the decision to check the ticket in the newspaper and what page the paper ended open at were all meant to happen...to give him confirmatory evidence that he *should* apply for the job that he had been mulling over for years."

Michael thought about Doc's explanation. "Yeah, ok, but which little event did you orchestrate?" His question was a test.

"Having the paper land open at that exact page. If he hadn't bought the lottery ticket or hadn't checked it in the newspaper, then my sign prodding him to apply for that new job would have had to have come about differently. My job, in this case, was to convince him to apply for that job change he had been contemplating for ten years. However, he did buy the ticket and he did throw the paper on the floor in disappointment. I saw my opportunity and went to work. Now, for his part. He has to see that ad and act on it. Remember I said that we just send signs and the Ones Below have to act on it. Well, there's an example."

"Or, I might arrange that my One Below meets a certain person at a crucial time in their life in the hopes that they will take something positive from the meeting and use that meeting to maybe bring them one step closer to their destination."

"So, your open papers and planned meetings will change people's lives...just like that? Is that what you mean?"

"Sure...kind of. In this case, it's not necessarily the event or the meeting of someone that will, in and of itself, change the person's life. No, it's how that person *reacts* to the event. It's how they allow that event to influence them and how they act subsequent to the event that will set in motion a new chain of events capable of altering their life for the better. So, like we've discussed before, the person has to be open to the fact that this event happened for a reason. From there, they have to be able to understand why it happened. After that, if they so choose, they have to act accordingly and in such a fashion that their new direction will bring about positive change. Their new direction...*that* will be the reason for their new-found lease on life. It's how they react to things that will chart the course for the future. Follow me, Michael?"

"Uh, huh."

"That's good...I just hope my assignment does."

"Very good my boy...well done indeed," said Michael. "You and your assignment will do just fine. It might take time—patience, as it were—but after a while, I'm sure you two will make a great team."

"A great team, that derives its strength and believes that good things come from God, you mean?"

"Yes, a team that has its success rooted in the belief of God...that's what I mean...well done again, my boy. So, you've really come to espouse the benefit of patience when it comes to how people Below should life their lives and it's not just because of some academic argument, is that right?"

"Absolutely," replied Doc. "Life Below in some respects is like a chess game. In order to win in chess and in life you have to set yourself up for success well in advance. You have to point yourself—or your chess pieces—in the right direction. Reaching your destiny or checkmating your opponent doesn't come in one move. You have to plan and work towards it. And, when life—or your opponent—throws an obstacle in your path, you have to regroup, exercise patience and plan again. You still strive for success but it might come on a different path. But make no mistake, success will come if you strive for it and keep yourself pointing in a relatively positive direction, being always at the ready to seize opportunities that may come your way. People who want to reach their destiny must strive, Michael. Everybody who strives will see their destiny come true."

28

ROMANS 12:1-2

Doc hadn't finished his summation.

"Striving is one of the qualities that Seekers possess. It's an important quality, but it's only one of many important qualities that set Seekers apart from others," said Doc, almost startled at his last sentence.

Michael was shocked. He knew over the course of their Interviews that Doc hadn't quite figured out what a Seeker was or what qualities Seekers possessed, so he was somewhat surprised that Doc offered his answer without even being asked or prompted for it. "Whoa, whoa, whoa...striving is one of the qualities of a Seeker? Is that what you said?"

"Yeah...why?"

"When did you figure out this little thingamajiggie? Have you been holding out on me?"

"No...honest. I just figured it out the other day down at the lake, honest. She's so smart, you know. Always knowing just the right questions to ask in order to get me to think."

"She?"

"Yeah, my lake."

"*Your lake?*"

"Yeah, my lake."

"Whatever... we can talk about your lake later...maybe you can take me to *your* lake one day, but for now, let's get back to Seekers. Ok, Seekers...what are they striving for?" asked Michael plainly, not wanting to make too big of a deal out of something that was a huge deal.

"Their destiny," replied Doc confidently. "Or, put another way, I suppose you could say, their purpose. Like, what gives their life meaning."

"Well, what's the difference between someone who just has a goal in mind and goes after it and a Seeker who follows the path to their destiny?"

"God."

"God?" asked Michael. "What's God got to do with someone's goal?"

"Everything. Well, He's got everything to do with a Seeker's destiny... and there is no greater kind...the destiny of a Seeker, that is," said Doc with more authority than he had ever spoken with before. "The destiny of a Seeker is rooted in their striving. Striving to see God's will done. His will, is their destiny. It can be as a professional athlete, a miner or a weatherman. It doesn't matter."

"I'm listening," said the Archangel, who was now very, *very* eager to hear Doc's idea of what a Seeker was and what was so special about a Seeker's destiny. "Go on."

"Well, for starters, a Seeker's belief in the team has no equal. They know the power of God and they know that He has assigned a Guardian Angel to help them on their quest to their destiny. You know, someone to send signs or help with burdens or temptations along the way if things get rough. God, to a Seeker, is very powerful...*all* powerful. Remember Michael, God is as powerful or powerless as the person Below will permit. Seekers, understanding God's benevolence and His yearning for them to succeed, choose to make Him as powerful as possible. It's entirely their decision."

"I'm with you so far. Keep going."

"Seekers have basically put their destinies in God's hands. They point themselves in a relatively positive direction and allow life, God and us, to show them the way. Of course, neither God nor we micro-manage their everyday life for them, but they have, in a way, let go of the reins or control of their life as it were, and have put their journey enroute to their destiny under the captaincy of God. To do that, they must believe that God will not lead them astray. And He won't. How can He...the Seeker is doing His will."

"God will look after them, will He?"

"Yes He will. He will shoulder burdens and take any earthly pain away they experience along their path to their true destiny. And, when the time is right, every single Seeker will reach their destiny. Their true destiny. Because it's God's will. It won't be as a person laden with debt or working at a barely tolerable job, which might very well be the destiny of some Below. No, they will reach their *true* destiny. Why will it be their true destiny? Because that's exactly the destination that God had planned for them and it will be great. It will be God's will. And, it will be Pure Joy."

Doc didn't stop. "Their path will be protected by us, as ordered by God and we will help them along that path—even though they don't know, nor do we, where that path will lead them."

Michael listened intently and nodded in agreement. Even Edmund, who had returned from stashing the seeds in his hole, was listening to Doc with wide eyes.

"The Seeker will not only experience earthly happiness—which is open to all Below—but they will also experience spiritual or inner happiness. In their soul. Happiness experienced by all who are following their destinies in a troupe of three, knows no equal. And *that* is Pure Joy."

Michael had only mentioned Pure Joy once or twice before in his conversations with Doc and he really wasn't sure whether Doc would come to understand the meaning of it during the course of the Interviews. Sometimes it takes Seniors months and years after having carriage of their new assignment to truly understand the meaning of Pure Joy.

"This Pure Joy you speak of, what do you mean by it?"

"It takes on different meanings, I suppose…but it only comes about when the One Below is following their destiny—their true destiny—hand in hand and step by step with God and their Guardian Angel. Reaching someone's true destiny is Pure Joy because it's the destiny He had always hoped they would find. It's part of His plan. His will. Existers and Blamers can live their life out only knowing their earthly destiny—that is, the destiny they've fabricated for themselves. If God didn't have a hand in it, then it's just that…an earthly destiny. Some obviously are satisfied with that. Seekers are not. They are not after their earthly destiny—one crafted by them alone. They are after their true destiny…the destiny God had hoped they would reach, planned only for them. They are after their final destination as planned by God. So, the final destination is Pure Joy; that is, it's Pure Joy knowing that your destination on earth is the destination that God had planned for you. That is your true destiny and it's Pure Joy."

"You said Pure Joy takes on possibly different meanings…there's more?" asked Michael.

"Sure. The *happiness* that one experiences along the way can also be described as Pure Joy. This happiness, or inner happiness as it were, is a deeper happiness than an earthly or material happiness. Happiness in the form of Pure Joy is only experienced by Seekers because it's the happiness that has as its root something deeper than material happiness…its roots are in God. There is no greater happiness…experienced along the journey and when realizing your true destiny."

Not quite finished yet, Doc continued. "And the Seeker's *journey* to the destination is also one of Pure Joy apart from the happiness that the journey itself brings. When One Below and their Guardian Angel are in sync and both are on the path to the true destiny that God has chosen for them, then that in itself is Pure Joy. Every member of the team feels it. Pure Joy permeates the team: God smiles because the One Below has allowed Him to be powerful; the Guardian Angels smile because they know that they have a hand in helping the One Below on their journey; people Below smile because they know that they are on the path to a destiny picked for them by God and not just some destination that they happened to find themselves at. And, for the One Below it's Pure Joy knowing that *they* are making God smile and are actually having a hand in doing God's will."

"People Below do God's will? Doesn't God do God's will?" asked Michael. "How do you know this…is this just your view of things or can someone back you up…like, say, Marco perhaps or another knowledgeable Advanced?"

"Sure, people do God's will. No, I don't have any other person, as it were, to back me up. Just God."

"God?"

"Yeah…God."

"You spoke to Him? You spoke to God?"

"No, I read it."

"You read one of God's writings?"

"No, Paul's. He wrote it, I just read it. So yeah, people do do God's will. Is that backing enough for you?"

"Yup."

"Aaaanyway, as I was reading Our Book the other day…and I know how picky you are about us Seniors being up on our Scripture readings…I came across this verse at Romans 12: 1-2. In part, it goes something like this:

…present your bodies a living and holy sacrifice, acceptable to God....and do not be conformed to this world, but be transformed by the renewing of your mind, that you may prove what the will of God is, that which is good and acceptable and perfect...

"That," said Doc, "the renewing of your mind to such an extent that it is acceptable to God will be Pure Joy. Their true destiny will be the will of God and that will be Pure Joy."

"Ok, but what's the meaning of this quote, or rather, how do people Below go about doing this?" Michael asked Doc, marvelling that no Senior had figured out the meaning of Pure Joy *before* their Senior assignment had started. Usually, everything fell into place only *after* their assignment was well on their path to realizing their true destiny—that which is God's will.

"Well, the person Below *really* has to believe in God. They have to believe to such an extent that they are comfortable with letting go of the reins of their life and the direction of their life so that it can be placed in God's hands. And that doesn't mean that they have to go to church seven times a week or join some fundamentalist cult or preach on the street corner. Heck, they don't even have to tell anyone they're doing it. Because what they're doing—allowing God to lead them for a bit or forever—is between them and God. No one need know. Aaaaanyway, once they really believe in the team and point themselves in a relatively positive direction—God and life will look after the rest."

"Anything else?" asked the Archangel.

"Kind of," continued Doc. "Paul, the author of the Book of Romans, asks people not to be concerned with this world so much—that is, their world Below—but rather they have to renew their mind—like, let go of the reins—in order to see God's will done. A will that is good, acceptable and perfect. The renewing of their mind takes on the same meaning as buying into the team. It's not hard, Michael, but it does take faith and...patience. And, at the end of it all, the person Below will reach their true destiny—not their earthly, engineered destiny—and it will be Pure Joy. Proving God's will, just like Paul said in Romans, will be the Pure Joy. I can't explain it any better than that."

The Archangel still had to appear stoic and officious in front of his student, but inside he was overjoyed…elated. Never before had a Senior showed so much eagerness to learn and never before had a Senior gleaned as much knowledge from his Observational Periods as Doc had. The consensus around the Academy and the Inner Circle was right—Doc was destined for great things…and so too would his new assignment Below.

For a moment, after Doc had finished his explaining about signs, Seekers, destinies and Pure Joy, both Guardian Angels sat side by side on the bench smiling silently looking out over the Main Path, its surrounding grass and towering trees. Doc knew what Michael was thinking and Michael knew what Doc was thinking. They were conversing through the art of unspoken communication. Doc knew that Michael was pleased with Doc's progress and Michael knew that Doc was very proud indeed for having unlocked the key to Pure Joy.

Michael chuckled and shook his head in disbelief at Doc's wisdom. Doc chuckled and shook his head in disbelief that he actually figured it out. He didn't see what the fuss over him was about; he just saw himself as a regular guy, an equal to others. *Pare inter pares.*

29

DOC as SENIOR

The Archangel was impressed with how Doc explained the things he had learned. "Say, throughout all your observations, I've heard you compare life to a revolving door, a chess game, baking a cake and bunch of other things as well. It's as if you've turned what you've learned into the art of teaching using parables. You, um...haven't been getting tutoring on the side from someone, have you?" Michael asked nervously, thinking that maybe Doc had been doing most of his learning under the hand of someone other than him.

Doc grinned. "Na, just you Michael...and my lake."

After a couple minutes of talking silently, Michael spoke.

"Doc," he began, "you've done an excellent job. You have learned more than I imagined and you understand what you have learned more than I had hoped. Well done indeed, my boy."

Doc looked at the Archangel and just smiled and nodded a single nod. And, after a moment said, "Thanks."

"Doc, my son, you have just passed your Senior Observational Interviews…in record time. After four Interviews, it is my pleasure to officially announce that you are no longer 'Doc, Senior Candidate,' but from here on in you are 'Doc, Senior Guardian Angel.' Congratulations."

Again, Doc just smiled at first. And again, after a moment, his words to his mentor were simple. "Thank you," said Doc as he reached out his hand to shake the Archangel's already outstretched.

As they shook hands, both Guardian Angels knew that the end of the Observational Interviews was just the beginning of an unshakeable, unassailable friendship. A friendship both would cherish even though they might not see the other as often as they would like—and one that would endure forever. True friendships didn't need daily affirmation. Through trials and good times or over years and years, true friendships lasted. They stuck.

"Now," said Michael reverting back to his old, carefree way, "I suppose we gotta get you a new assignment, huh? It won't do having our latest Senior sitting around idly now, will it? Sitting around idly might just find you at the euchre game over at Gallery 97, eh?"

"Well, actually, I had thought about throwing a hand or two, but that can wait. There will be more games…patience, right?" asked Doc smiling.

"Yes, no doubt you'll find a game over the next little bit…I imagine your friends at 97 will be anxious to hear how you made out too…anyway, that can wait. How about we meet tomorrow and I'll give you your new assignment then? I should double-check the list to make sure I've got it right. Besides, I'm not entirely sure an assignment has even been picked out yet. I know there was a few short-listed, but I don't know if it was ever decided which one it would be. After all, most of the Academy and the Inner Circle figured you would take five…or six Interviews…not four. I guess they've been caught a little unawares, if you will. Come to think of it, I think a few members of the Academy and the Inner Circle lost a bit of money."

Doc didn't understand.

"Oh, there were a few friendly wagers being placed on how many Interviews it would take you."

"Ohhhh, I seeeee," said Doc with a smirk, "so it's not just the gang down at Gallery 97 that partake in hazardous games?"

Embarrassed and turning red, Michael lowered his head and said with a smile, "No, I guess not. Not a word, my boy. This information…keep it secret, keep it safe."

"Wagering, what wagering?" Doc said with a knowing wink.

"There…that's a good Senior, now about tomorrow…" started Michael before Doc interjected.

"Tell me, Michael, how did *you* fare in the betting?"

"How do you know I bet anything?" said the Archangel who now was turning beet red.

"Because I've come to know your mischievous ways, that's how I know…so, how did you fare?"

Michael looked around to see if anyone was in earshot. He then looked back at Doc. "Uh, actually, my money was on four Interviews…most of the others owe me," Michael said with a boyish grin flashing across his face and a satisfying chuckle.

"Is that not a conflict of interest?" asked Doc with a semi-serious look. "After all, could you not have passed me with four Interviews just to win?"

"Doc, Senior Guardian Angel!" exclaimed Michael. "I'm shocked that such a thought would even enter your mind. I do my work with complete impartiality and without the slightest scintilla of bias," he said half sternly. "I am above reproach. The others know this and besides they knew full well it was I who was conducting your Interviews. They dare not impugn the integrity of the Archangel! There's only One who has the moral authority to do that. And we didn't bring Him in on this wager…He wins too much. Besides,

I'm donating all my winnings to the refurbishing of the Pearly Gates…so there."

Both Angels shared a laugh. Even Edmund seemed to be enjoying the lively discussion.

"So," continued Michael, "tomorrow…same place, same time?"

"As usual," Doc said as he rose from the bench. "And Michael, thanks again. I appreciate everything you taught me. It was fun learning from you."

"Well thank you, Doc, but it was you that did the learning…I just prodded now and again."

As the three of them walked away, Doc knew that his success as a student was in part due to how Michael inspired him to learn and Michael knew that his success as a teacher was in part due to how Doc inspired him to teach.

30

a seekeʀ ʜe ɡets

Both Angels arrived at exactly the same time and both were right on time. Finally, they were in sync.

"Morning, Senior," Michael said with a smile.

"Morning, Michael," replied Doc.

"So, ready to find out who your assignment is?"

"I could hardly sleep last night...wondering who I would get kept me up most of the night."

Without further banter, the Archangel, a little edgy, got right down to business.

"Well, wait no longer, my boy. You have a Blamer...a brand new Blamer too—like, about five minutes ago. He has only minutes ago expressed his belief in God, thus acquiring himself a Guardian. It's a tenuous belief, but a belief nonetheless."

Doc just looked at Michael dumbfounded. He didn't speak. Then, Doc turned and looked straight ahead off into the distance.

Still a little uneasy, Michael kept going. "Seems that your new One Below has just become a fair-weather-believer-in-times-of-crisis...apparently, someone close to him died and for the first time in his life he asked God to look after them while they were up Here. Never before had this person expressed a belief in God. It just happened. Like...just happened."

Doc was speechless. He thought he was getting a Seeker. Someone who had bought into the team and someone who Doc could really guide and teach. Someone who needed the services of a good Senior; someone who would listen and heed the signs. Besides, Doc was always told he might get a Seeker. He looked back at Michael with a look of astonishment, still not uttering a word. Doc was devastated.

"Yeah, tell me about it. This was a surprise to me too. Apparently, this guy Below, out of the blue and all of a sudden says to God...oh, and by the way, this new One Below of yours, not only didn't believe in God prior to today, but he was emphatic about His non-existence...anyway, as soon as he prayed to God to look after his departed friend, God immediately called me. And don't forget, this happened as I was walking here. I had already been to the Academy's administrative office to see who it was that had been assigned and I was walking here to tell you who it was."

Doc listened, but still said nothing.

"Yeah, so anyway, I'm walking here," continued Michael, "and He starts calling me, so I rush over to Him and we start talking about who your new assignment is. I told Him who it was and then a discussion ensued and, well, to make a long story short...by the end of it all you had a new, different assignment."

Doc listened, but still said nothing.

"Doc, dude, I know you were after a Seeker and I know you were really looking forward to guiding someone who was going to be open to your signs and opportunities, but Doc...this is just the way things are. Expect the unexpected. It's a personal assignment from God. It just doesn't get any better than that."

Completely dejected and in tears, Doc finally spoke.

"Yeah, it doesn't get any better *or harder*. Michael...I've seen these Blamers. They're stuck...they live on cruise control...they blame everyone for their lot in life...they never get to see the future because they never live it. Their present is always the past; their future is always the present...which brings them back to the past. Michael, Blamers never amount to anything. I know. I've seen them. Damn it, Michael. This is horse-shit and you know it. You're the Archangel and all you could get for me was a stupid Blamer. Thanks, Michael. I deserve better. I know I deserve better. Bloody horse-shit is what it is."

Both Angels sat silent for a moment. Michael knew that Doc needed a moment's delay to calm down. Doc knew he needed a moment's delay to quit seeing red.

After a minute or two of allowing Doc to cool down a bit, Michael thought he might as well get the rest of the news over with as well.

"Not only is your One Below only a new fair-weather-believer-in-times-of-crisis and an expert Blamer, but he's also unemployed... or soon will be and he's in debt up to his eyeballs. Oh, and uh...he hangs out with a bunch of criminals. His friends that aren't criminals are Existers. And just so you know, apparently he became a Blamer in his early twenties. So he's had about ten years of a head start on any guiding you might want to do. Dropping out of university, he blamed his professors for his poor marks. His parents for an awful upbringing...which isn't true by the way. He blamed an ex-girlfriend for destroying his life when she found someone who treated her better. And, somewhere along the way, I think he blamed his dog for dying on him. Some of those details are a little fuzzy...I had not but a moment or two to read his sheet."

But Michael was saving the best for last. He decided that he wouldn't tell Doc what else he knew until this first stuff had soaked in. Michael knew that this would be an initial blow to Doc because he was so looking forward to receiving a Seeker. Someone with whom he could really do great stuff with. Michael wanted to make sure that Doc understood the true character of his new assignment. Only then could Doc really understand the significance and the meaning of his new assignment Below.

"But, Michael," Doc pleaded, "I can't get a Blamer. They don't do anything but blame. They live their entire life blaming. I'm supposed to get a Seeker. You said yourself that I might get one. Can't you do anything about it?" said Doc as he looked at Michael with exasperation. His tears returned.

"Well, wasn't it you who said," retorted Michael, as he remembered some of their earlier conversations, "that it was always open for these people to change? That they didn't have to stay an Exister or Blamer their entire life. Isn't that what you said?"

"Yes, that's what I said, but I also came to the conclusion, as did you, that it might very well be the destiny of these people to also end their lives as Existers and Blamers and not knowing anything but."

Doc was beside himself. How could he put to use all the good skills he learned during his Interviews if his new assignment cared not one bit for the team nor was open to receiving, interpreting and acting on signs. Things didn't happen for a reason to a Blamer…they just happened.

"Uh, huh," Michael agreed, "yes, the destiny of Existers and Blamers can be just that. That is, yes, they could finish out their days without joining the Content or knowing of the team to become a Seeker. But I don't think that will be your new assignment's destiny. Nor yours to idly look after a Blamer."

"Whatever, Michael," Doc said, half listening and half staring off to wherever.

"No, Doc," Michael said quietly, "the destiny of your Blamer…" He paused until Doc had finished his staring at nothing and returned to the conversation, "…the destiny of your Blamer, is to be a Seeker." Michael waited for Doc's reaction. "And you must see to it."

Doc just looked at the Archangel.

A Seeker? My Blamer, who just barely believes in God, who is in debt, who hangs with criminals and has no job...yeah, *he's* going to be a Seeker.

"Sure, Michael, and I'm Michelangelo. No wait, even better, I'm the Queen of England. Yes, that's it. Oh, did you not know? I *am* the Queen of England. Take your pick out of the lot of them. Elizabeth or Victoria, I don't care. You pick. I'm her. Whatever dude. Say what you want. Michael, for a Blamer to become a Seeker is a one-in-a-million chance...my guy with the lottery ticket has a better chance at winning. Blamers don't care for improving their lot. In order for a Blamer to become a Seeker, it would take..." Doc said, as he thought for a moment until he had something that he could finish off his sentence with a bang, "...yes, in order for a Blamer to become a Seeker...it would...it would, take an act of God."

Doc looked at Michael.

Michael looked at Doc.

Neither spoke.

Realizing what he had just said, Doc's eyes opened up in amazement and he turned back to stare at the nothing that he had been looking out at before. But this time, instead of staring with empty eyes and empty thoughts, his thoughts were full and his eyes sparkled. And the nothing he stared out at was now something. Something filled with promise and challenge.

An act of God, thought Doc.

Michael laughed on the inside. Give this boy a moment or two and he usually figures things out on his own. I have no idea what this Blamer did to deserve Doc, but for some reason he lucked out. Obviously God sees something in Doc's new One Below and wanted him to have the very best chance at success.

After a moment had passed, Doc spoke...almost embarrassed.

"Wow," said Doc. It was all he could manage to squeak out.

"Yeah...wow is right."

"Listen, ah, about that Archangel bit and you not being able to get me someone better and the horse-shit stuff, uh, I really didn't mean it…no offence."

Michael felt like laughing, but contained it in a serious look. He looked at Doc from under his hair that had fallen down in front of his face when he turned to Doc in disbelief when Doc mentioned the horse thing. "None taken. And by the way, horses have nothing to do with it…just so you're clear. In a case like this, bulls would seem more appropriate."

Michael knew that God saw this Blamer would turn his life around and He wanted to assign the best to ensure that he got to his destination…his destiny of Pure Joy. For Doc, it meant being given great responsibility by the Almighty…maybe too soon.

"Michael," Doc said with a shaky voice, "I don't think I'm ready. In fact, I *know* I'm not ready. I was ready for a Seeker…someone who embraced God and who would look skyward for answers and guidance. I'm not sure if I'm ready to guide the unguidable."

"Hmmm…that's funny," said Michael. "He thinks you're ready. So do I. I guess that means you're wrong. Oh, and one more thing, what you think really is beside the point. In case you haven't noticed it's what *He* thinks that matters. About everything."

"I hope He knows what He's doing."

"I think He does. Don't forget it is your new assignment's *ultimate* destiny to be a Seeker in the future. It's *not* his destiny to be a Seeker today, nor tomorrow, nor even by next month or year. Life destinies take time, Doc. God's will take time. You know this. It takes patience. And all your One Below has is time. True, his journey—and yours—will be long and at times frustrating and it might even seem to him Below pointless. But you must not lose faith. Neither must he."

"Patience," said Doc. "I know, it's the key. I've said it myself."

"Do you believe your own words, Doc?"

Doc paused for a moment before he answered. "Yeah, I believe them."

"Great…that's all I needed to hear. You two will do just fine. Just remember, your new One Below is not ready to be a Seeker overnight and you aren't ready yet to guide him there overnight. It might take years of trial and error. But so long as you both believe in the team, the two of you will reach that destination. Reaching it will be Pure Joy for everybody. And I would guess that in a few years when you two are clicking and are in sync...well, that journey will be Pure Joy too."

"I suppose so."

"Suppose nothing. When he does reach his personal destiny, he will be seen as a success story down Below and up Here you will be seen as a Genius. Imagine, helping a Blamer become a Seeker. It doesn't get any better than that, Doc."

"Yeah, it doesn't get any better, or like I said before, it doesn't get any harder than that either."

"Sure it'll be tough, Doc. But hey, tough times don't last...tough people do. Doc, you are going to be a great Guardian Angel for your new One Below, that I know. But he's learning and so are you. Success for each of you will come in time. The only one on the team who doesn't have to learn anything new is God and He already knows that both of you will succeed. He knows that his person Below will end up a Seeker. He's already updated The Parchment. Perhaps one of the reasons why He knows your assignment will find his true destiny...the destiny of a Seeker...might be the fact that He has assigned you to help him on his journey. Did you ever think about that?"

"No...but I suppose you're right."

"Suppose has nothing to do with it," said Michael. "God only assigns the best Seniors to the hardest of journeys. It is true, that most Senior's get Seekers, because they've already bought into the team and the vast knowledge of the Senior can help them get one step closer to their true destiny. But when God sees that there's a one-in-a-million Blamer who, in the future, will buy into the team and will keep striving, well, then He also assigns a Senior because He knows that the Senior will be best able to help that person on their long journey."

"What if I fail? What if I let you and God down?"

"You won't. Neither will your assignment. It's natural to be nervous about such huge challenges the first time around. Heck, even brain surgery and flying is hard the first time, but the brain surgeons and pilots get used to it. So will you."

"But Michael, most Seekers have already learned the value of pointing themselves in a relatively positive direction and thereby have come to believe that things always work themselves out in the end...and if things aren't right at a particular moment in time, then they know that the end hasn't come yet."

Doc sat silent for a moment. He was searching for something, for an answer. For a starting point where he would first take his new One Below.

"Hmm," Doc started out. "I guess my first job will be to see to it that my One Below points himself in a relatively positive direction. That's all I have to do. Get him to point himself in a relatively positive direction and everything else will fall into place. Yes, that's the first thing I must do." Doc was starting to feel better about his challenge.

Michael smiled. Doc never seemed to disappoint. Here Doc was only moments earlier doubting his capabilities and within a few short minutes he was already deciding what it was that he must do first in order to help his One Below. "That's good, Doc. That's good. I think that would be a great place to start. Help him point himself in a relatively positive direction and help him understand that things will work out for him if he lets them. From there, you guys can work on patience and happiness."

Doc sighed. "Seems I have my work cut out for me, huh? Oh well, I'm up for the challenge. Yes, I'm starting to feel quite good about all this now. Michael, just so you know, I'm going to strive to be the best Guardian Angel I can be. And in doing so, I'll do everything I can to help my new One Below. Most of the striving will be up to him but perhaps I can lessen his burden now and again. After all, God will lessen burdens and temptations to those so afflicted...I'll just try and help him seize those opportunities."

Doc would be striving once again and Michael knew it. Doc was a striver, regardless of the task at hand.

"Yes, I will strive to help him the best I can and I will also keep striving to learn as much as I can," said Doc with a sense of conviction. "I remember you saying during our very first chat that God will always let people everywhere, in every form of existence, prove their worth. Well, I'm going to prove my worth. You just wait and see."

Michael kept smiling at Doc. Yes Doc, he said to himself, you keep striving. "And Doc," the Archangel began quietly, "you *do* keep striving because you have a destiny to reach up Here too, you know. Keep striving up Here and Pure Joy will be yours once more…only it's a tad better than the Pure Joy experienced Below. Strive, Doc."

That made Doc very happy. You just wait, Michael, Doc said silently to the Archangel as they sat quietly enjoying the moment, my new One Below and I will make a great team. Me and…hey, I don't know this guy's name yet. "So, what's my new assignment's name?"

"Name?" asked Michael.

"Yes, name," answered Doc. "What's my new assignment's name?"

"Ah yes…name," said Michael nervously.

He was stalling. He didn't get the name from God in his haste. Michael was briefed by God as to the change of assignment and in the excitement of it all he forgot to get the new assignment's name. "Of course, yes, name. The name of your new assignment is what you want. I can't believe I didn't say it at the outset."

The ceremony, thought Michael, that'll cover my tracks.

Covering his absentmindedness, Michael explained to Doc that he would get the name of his new assignment at the ceremony that afternoon, where the Academy and the Inner Circle would formally bestow Doc with the rank of Senior and officially welcome him as such.

"A ceremony?" Doc asked. "For me? I don't want a ceremony. Stuffy things. Nothing but pomp and circumstance…Uhhh, what time?" Doc added excitedly, betraying his supposed aloofness to the whole affair.

"Three o'clock, which is in about…one hour. Oh my gosh, that doesn't leave me much time to change," Michael said as he looked down his front and saw Edmund had left some slobber after one of his many feeding sessions.

"I better change too…these ripped jeans might not go over that well," said Doc excitedly.

"And the hat, Doc, please."

"Oh yeah…ok, I won't bring the hat."

"Thank you…see you at the Academy at 3:00…sharp!"

"As you wish."

31

ADVANCED

As their parting handshake was loosening, Doc spoke up.

"Just before you go, Michael, I've been wondering…if God ensures that Seniors are assigned to either Seekers or others that will become Seekers, who does He assign to Advanced? It seems that the best Guardian Angels should be assigned to them."

Michael replied in the most compassionate voice that Doc had yet heard him use.

"God assigns His best and most understanding Guardian Angels, the Advanced, to the elderly, the mentally ill and the disabled…His most beloved people Below."

Doc didn't answer, nor did Michael expect one. Their eyes met and they conversed briefly in silence…each knowing that God keeps His best helpers for the most needy.

"You'll get there Doc…just you wait," said Michael.

With that, both Angels went their way. But suddenly, Doc had another question. Turning around, he called after Michael. "Hey, before the last-minute change, who was my assignment supposed to be?"

Without turning around and without breaking stride, Michael spoke back. "A Seeker."

Spinning around and heading for home, Doc felt good. No matter, I'll have a Seeker soon enough…then, a grandmother.

32

garbage?

Doc rushed home and changed into something more appropriate for his official Senior welcoming ceremony. Off came his ripped jeans and hat. On went his dress kilt and jacket. Off came his dress kilt and jacket. On went his beige robe. Off came his beige robe.

I know, I'll put on the same clothes I was wearing the day I passed my Senior entrance exams…my good luck clothes. That was the same day I met Michael. What a great day!

On went his best white robe with the two silk-lined front pockets and cord sash.

With his new change of clothes, Doc was off to the Academy. He did not want to be late.

Close to the Academy grounds, Doc saw that a group of fellow

Seniors and some professors had already arrived and were enjoying the fresh air outside before the ceremony's commencement. Michael was there also. They waved as Doc approached.

Not but a hundred feet from the Academy, Doc felt something in his pocket. He stuck his hand in the pocket and felt his fingers fumble on something. From the feel of it he guessed it to be that old piece of scrap, discarded paper that was laying on the path near the bench where he and Michael had shared their very first chat months prior. Taking it for garbage, Doc remembered that he picked the piece of litter up so he could toss it in a garbage can.

As Doc drew closer to the front of the Academy, he made a quick detour just off to the right of The Main Path to a garbage can. As he threw the litter in the garbage can, he noticed that there was some writing on it. He peered in the can for a closer look and read four words as it lay on the bottom of the trash barrel.

He would never forget those four words. He would guide using those four words. He would live his own life Above following those four words. Doc picked the piece of litter up out of the can, put it back in his pocket and looked up towards Michael.

Flipping his hair out of the way, Michael flashed Doc his trademark smile.

As Doc walked towards Michael, Doc returned Michael's smile with a knowing nod. Life Above as a Senior would be good. It was time to get to work.

epilogue

Strive. Be a Seeker.

ACCORDING to *Maclean's* magazine 62% of Canadians believe in angels. So did C. S. Lewis.

C. S. Lewis, author of many books including *The Chronicles of Narnia: The Lion, the Witch and the Wardrobe,* wrote about an old, scheming devil giving a young devil tips on how to best able turn people away from God in his critically acclaimed novelette *The Screwtape Letters.*

However, Lewis always felt something was missing. He wrote,

> Ideally, Screwtape's advice should have been balanced by archangelical advice to the patient's guardian angel. Without this, the picture of human life is lop-sided. But who could supply the deficiency?

The Soul Listener provides the deficiency Lewis longed for.

The Soul Listener also provides what, deep-down, most Canadians also long for: advice, help, guidance and courage from their Guardian Angel.

The Soul Listener, with its playful yet controversial commentary on modern Western society will—better than the how-to-books, better than the self-help books—help the reader identify what it is that is preventing them from discovering their destiny. And then, it leads the reader to their own destiny…the purpose in one's life.

Readers gain a reflective yet provocative look at our own modern-day pop culture, the crippling effects of debt and obsession with gadgets, and what it is that can open the door for anyone to reach their destiny—the reason for being born.

Nothing else matters in life other than finding one's destiny.

Finding one's destiny won't happen in one day. It is a journey. Are you ready for a journey that will change your life?

The Soul Listener is destiny revealed for everyone… just what C. S. Lewis envisioned.

Printed in the United States
100835LV00002B